44

Book Five

Jools Sinclair

Praise for *44*...

44

Book Five

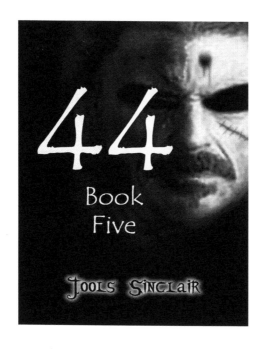

Jools Sinclair

You Come Too Publishing

44 Book Five

Published by You Come Too Publishing, Bend, Oregon.

Printed in the United States of America

First edition, 2012

ISBN-13: 978-1479181230
ISBN-10: 1479181234

For Mom,
This, and a thousand
lemon cake kisses...

Prologue

It was the noise that woke me.

I sat up, confused. I was in a chair, next to an empty bed. The curtains blowing in the wind.

Then I remembered.

She was sick, very sick.

I touched the sheets and glanced in the bathroom.

Where was she?

There it was again, coming from somewhere outside.

I walked to the window and let my eyes adjust to the darkness. And then I saw that someone was out there, near the fence by the flower garden. A black silhouette at the edge of the yard, moving. Something in his hands.

I ran and got the gun.

"Abby?" I whispered as I made my way down the hall.

There was no reply. She wasn't in the living room watching TV.

I hurried to the kitchen and froze. The sliding glass door was open, the cool air blowing in. My mouth went dry.

"Abby!" I said, trying to contain my fear.

Nothing.

"Let her be okay," I whispered and walked out to the patio, the gun out in front of me.

I released the safety and scanned the yard.

Just him.

He could be anyone. He could be one of them, coming back for her. I gathered my courage and steadied my hand as I moved toward the dark figure.

His back was to me. He was doing something. He had a shovel in this hands. He was digging.

"Stop!" I yelled, pointing the gun at his head.

He slowly turned around, the porch light catching his face. I gasped and dropped the gun.

She looked at me, her eyes fierce.

"I've been waiting for you," she said in a dead voice.

I backed away, staring at the ground, at what she had done. All the flowers were dug up and thrown to the side. Where there had been a garden there was now just a large hole in the ground.

"Abby, what are you doing?" I screamed.

She raised the shovel up over her head.

"Digging, Kate," she said, a smile spreading across her pale face. "I'm digging your grave."

Chapter 1

"I'm not sure how much more I can take," David said. "This town's not big enough for both of us."

He was going on about the director of the current production at 2nd Street Theater. David didn't get the lead and was given a minor role. He hadn't taken it well.

"And you know what he says to me? 'I saw your last performance and I think you might be better suited for musicals.' Musicals! Child, please. I hate musicals!"

"Bummer," Ty said.

While I didn't enjoy seeing David in pain, the timing of his theatrics was spot on. I was hoping it would distract people from what they were putting in their mouths. I had put a lot of effort into the dinner, but it hadn't come together. The chicken was dry and the gnocchi were rubbery.

"Sorry," I said when we had finished. "I'll do better next time."

We were sitting around the table in the backyard, under the willow with its long, cascading branches swaying gently around us.

"No," Ty said, reaching over and patting my arm. "It was good. Look, I finished everything on my plate. Really, it wasn't *that* bad, Abby."

I wondered if he was just being nice or if I had damaged his taste buds.

"I liked that salad dressing," David said with a sigh, leaning toward me and dropping his chin firmly on his fists. "It had a nice tart flavor that enhanced the lettuce beautifully."

"And those little tomatoes you used were something else," Lyle said.

"Those were Kate's contribution, fresh from her garden," I said.

I had been working in the kitchen for hours on my first day off in more than two weeks. I wanted it to be special. I wanted to impress Ty with an excellent home-cooked meal. I slowly drew in the warm evening air, reminding myself that cooking was an art and that this meal had turned out like a child's stick drawing.

I'm not sure what I had expected. I'd barely been in the kitchen in recent months. Between working as a river guide and at Back Street and playing soccer, I just didn't have the time. I was rusty and the proof was sitting in my stomach.

"Hey, don't forget the Chianti. It was amazing," David said, pouring himself another glass. "Besides, being here with all you special people was super fun."

I smiled.

"Here, here," Kate said as she lifted a glass for a toast. Everyone joined in.

"You're just lucky I'm not still with Eduardo," David went on. "I mean, that guy was ruthless when it came to food. One time we were at the Blacksmith and they had overdone his steak by a smidgen and he threw a complete fit. You know what I'm talking about, Ty. He was over at Ten Barrel sometimes."

"Yeah, I totally remember Eduardo," Ty said. "Nobody at work is missing him. He used to always complain about everything, but then he always came back for more."

"Tell me about it," David said, one eyebrow flying high up on his forehead.

Kate giggled, which sent David into hysterics for the next five minutes, complete with heavy wheezing and coughing.

I was glad he was feeling better.

I glanced back over at Ty. The soft glow of the fading sun was lighting up his face and his eyes were sparkling and clear, making the hairs on my arms stand up.

"Oh, hey," David said after he recovered. "I heard from Mo last night and the tour's been extended. She won't be back now until fall."

"That's awesome," I said.

"Lucky," Lyle said. "I sure wouldn't mind roaming around Europe all summer."

I was glad Lyle had been able to come. He worked with us over at Back Street as a part time barista and was a nature photographer the rest of the time. Some of his photos were displayed at the coffeehouse. His work was nice and peaceful, and lately, seemed to be focused exclusively on trees. They were quiet photos, which is probably why most people passed right by them, and why they didn't sell.

Besides his passion for photography, I didn't know much else about Lyle. He'd moved to Bend a few years ago from some small town in the Willamette Valley, and when we were closing together, he liked to play soft indie rock like Iron & Wine or Band of Horses. He was older, in his early 40's maybe. He wore his hair in a big, frizzy white man afro, and liked to wear flared jeans, like he was stuck in the era he was born in.

He wasn't a big talker, and when he did talk, he'd say odd things. He seemed to march to the beat of his own drummer, but it seemed like most of us at Back Street did in one way or another. He fit right in.

"I love what you guys have done to the place," Erin said.

It was good to see her again. She used to work with Kate at *The Bugler* and was staying with us for a few days. It had been a great week so far, especially at night when we all stayed up watching *Chopped* and *Sweet Genius*.

"Seriously, Kate? You built that pond?"

I loved the pond. Kate had put it in a few months ago, with lily pads, frogs, a few fish, and a waterfall. I especially liked to sit by it at night.

"Abby helped," Kate said.

"No, not much," I said.

We sat talking and laughing until the sun fell behind the trees. A chill came up.

"So what are we going to do later?" Ty asked.

"I don't care," I said. "Anything."

He smiled.

"How about a long walk?" he said. "Or maybe a movie?"

Even though we saw each other on the river most days, we really didn't see each other as much as we wanted. Ty was still working at Ten Barrel, and most nights he was either brewing beer or waiting tables. And although I had cut back on my hours at Back Street, I was still working there more than I had planned.

"Yeah, either one sounds good," I said. "I just need to clean up a little."

I looked out at the mess of dishes and after insisting that everybody stay seated, I got up and picked up as many as I could as David started in on the director again. Ty followed me to the kitchen with a huge stack of plates.

After we put them on the counter, he wrapped his arms around me and pulled me close, kissing me gently.

"I love you, Abby," he said, his breath heavy in my ear.

My stomach tightened, like it always did in these moments, the words in my head never making it down to my tongue. I smiled as I looked up into his serious eyes, trying to say something meaningful, trying to express how I felt.

But like always, I couldn't.

"Thanks," I said finally, killing the moment like a Spanish matador.

He smiled a little Charlie Brown smile and let me go.

"I'll get the rest," he said, a hint of sadness in his step as he walked back outside.

It had been the third time I had done that. The third time he had told me that he loved me and I wasn't able to tell him anything back. It wasn't because I didn't feel the same way. What I felt when I saw him for the first time in the morning or when we kissed was strong and real. I knew that I loved Ty. But there was something about saying it out loud, something about telling him and declaring it that I had trouble with. It felt impossible.

But when he returned with his arms full of glasses and bottles, he was happy again.

"Well, I still liked your dinner," he said. "I don't care what you say."

"Okay. But I'm hoping you will give me another chance. I'm so much better than this. Really, I am."

"Anytime. Just say the word."

I watched his bright energy dance around him and then hugged him, putting my head on his chest and listening to his heart, strong and steady.

Chapter 2

David came up behind me and whispered in my ear as I handed a customer his change. He was going through a health food phase, saying he needed to find a way to recover faster from all his partying. I could smell the mix of alcohol coming off his skin along with the spinach-celery smoothie on his breath.

"Don't freak out, Abby Craig," he said, "but she's in here again."

I wasn't going to freak out. I had promised myself once I had started sleeping better a few months ago that I was going to be more easy about everything. More than most people my age, I had come face to face with the end of the world. I had died and come back to life. I had dealt with the death of my mom and Jesse. I had been kidnapped and my kidnapper had tried to kill me. I knew a little about life and death. Most things were not the end of the world.

"Over there," he said, his eyes bugging as he shifted them back and forth trying to get me to look in her direction. "The one wearing the pink T-shirt."

I sighed. There were a few women sitting by themselves in the café wearing T-shirts so I had no idea who he was talking about.

"Oops," he said. "My bad. Sorry! I'm always forgetting that you can't see any colors. Okay, the girl sitting by the window with the short dark hair. The one who looks like she got up on the wrong side of the bed, all moody and such."

I found her. She was probably in her late twenties. She sucked on a straw as she stared out the window. And she did look serious.

"What do you think she wants?" I asked after I rang up another order.

"Don't know," David said. "But the lady is determined. She's been in here three times this week asking for you. You were in the back getting the cups when she came in a few minutes ago, but I already told her you were here and that you'd be out soon."

"Way to go," I said.

"What? I should lie?"

He poured some coffee that had just finished brewing and handed it to me.

"I got the counter covered if you want to take a few minutes."

"Thanks," I said.

After I had helped stop the school bombing in May, I had been labeled "Dream Girl" by the press and my story, name, and face had been plastered all over the place. Reporters wanted interviews, strangers wrote asking for help finding a lost loved one, and local parents thanked me with tears in their eyes. The excitement lasted for a few weeks. I finally became old news when Hollywood's hottest young couple called it quits.

A detective from the Bend Police Department still showed up at Back Street from time to time, always with a few "new" questions, questions I had already answered dozens of times about how I knew that a student was bringing a bomb to his high school that day. He wasn't satisfied that it was a psychic vision that had helped stop Devin Cypher from killing hundreds of people.

"David," I whispered. "Tell me again what you know. What did she say exactly?"

He leaned his back against the pastry case, folded his arms across his chest, and looked up at the ceiling.

"It's filthy up there," he said. "I mean, would you look at those cobwebs."

"David, focus."

"She asked for Abby," he said, still looking up and making a face. "That's it. She first came in Monday. Or maybe it was Tuesday. Anyway it was early afternoon and she made it a point to come up to me to ask if you were working. She walked right past Lyle. Then yesterday, same time, just after noon. Same thing, completely ignored Mike. It's like she knows we're friends or something. So that's when I told her that you are out on the river all day and that she would have to come back after five o'clock to find you. I asked her if she wanted me to give you a message, but she said no, that she wanted to speak with you. That's it."

I picked up my coffee.

"Now that I think about it, she does look awfully familiar," he said. "Maybe I've seen her on TV before, like a news show or something. But I don't know. She doesn't seem like a reporter to me. Your sister would never be caught dead in those flip flops and cut offs. On or off the job."

I guess there was one thing I already knew about her. If David was able to see her, the woman by the window wasn't a ghost.

"Cowboy up," I said to myself.

"Go get her and remember I'm right here," David said. "Just holler if you need me."

"I feel so safe just knowing that."

"Don't be snide, Abby Craig."

She still seemed lost in thought. A deep line formed between her large dark eyes when she noticed me standing over her. She squinted and then nodded without speaking. Her energy was gray and turbulent, crashing all around her.

"Abby Craig," I said, sitting across from her.

"Paloma Suárez," she said, the corners of her mouth turning up slightly in a weak attempt at a smile.

"David said you were looking for me."

"Yeah, thanks for coming over. I'm sorry to bother you, but he said you might be able to help."

"He?" I said, confused.

"David. Didn't he tell you?"

"No, he just said you've come in a few times and asked for me. Anyway, I don't have much time. I'm on my break."

The people behind us got up and left and suddenly it was quieter in the café.

She seemed nervous, playing with the paper wrapper from her straw. She didn't give off the type of vibe I had learned to associate with reporters or cops. I didn't know what she wanted but her anxiety left me feeling more re-laxed. I eased back in my chair and waited.

"So, uh, David, he didn't get a chance to tell you about my problem?" she said finally.

"No," I said, glancing back over at him.

He was lingering at the counter, all ears. When he caught me staring at him, he gave me a thumbs up and threw his towel up over his shoulder and looked away.

"*Cabrón*," she said loudly, her eyes moving from me to him and back again.

"So you told David your problem?"

"Well, I guess I just mentioned it casually. He comes into the club where I work pretty regularly. I was serving him last week and I told him about this, this, uh, situation I was having and he suggested that I talk to you."

"What kind of situation?" I asked.

She lowered her voice.

"Look, I want you to know I don't believe in it," she said. "No offense and all, but I don't believe in your *brujo* shit, Abby. I stopped going to church a long time ago and I never got around to replacing it with some *gringo* paranormal belief system."

"Okay," I said slowly, not knowing what else to say or sure what she was talking about.

What I was sure of, however, was that David had gotten a little too much sauce in him and spilled all over the sides about me. And just when things had started to quiet down. I was also sure that a health food hadn't been discovered yet that would help him recover from the neck wringing I was going to give him. Of course she looked familiar to David. She was his damn bartender.

"Ever notice how all those shows about ghosts only have white people being haunted?" she said, looking out the window. "Well, I guess I'm here to bring a little balance to things."

I still didn't know what she wanted from me.

"I don't know what else to think, except that I'm going crazy," she whispered, now looking deep into my eyes. "But I think it's happening to me. I think I'm… I'm being haunted."

I didn't say anything.

"David said he had a good friend who was a ghost hunter. He was supposed to ask if this was okay, me talking to you. But I think he's blowing me off, acting like he doesn't even know me. I didn't know what else to do."

I wondered if he was too embarrassed over having told her about me or if he really didn't remember. If he had just blabbed out and then blacked out.

"That's okay," I said. "But I still don't know what you what me to do. Or what I can do."

Jesse's words buzzed around my brain about how I needed to protect myself, how I couldn't help everybody and that there were a million ghosts out there that would want something from me.

"I really don't know where else to turn, Abby," she said. "Or who else to ask. None of this makes sense to me. Like I said, I don't even believe in ghosts. Look, I can pay you. I just need help. I think it's getting worse. I see him every night now."

"Who?" I said.

She was looking out the window again.

"What's that black rock all over the street?" she asked, her voice low and raspy. "When did they do that? Must help with the mud in winter."

I looked outside. I couldn't see what she was talking about. The asphalt?

"Who do you see every night, Paloma?" I said.

She looked at me again.

"Huh? Oh, he hangs out at the club. This guy, this spirit or whatever, he just stares at me. At first I thought he was real, I mean, human. You know, just a creep. I tried to have the bouncer throw out his ass. But no one else sees him. Just me."

It began in her eyes. The terror. They started to dance wildly. And then it swamped her like a canoe in a windstorm. She started shaking, the ice rattling in the clear plastic cup before she could put it down, her voice quivering.

"Sorry," she said as she looked down and ran her trembling hands through her short hair. "I haven't been able to sleep in weeks. I know you don't know me from Adam's house cat, but this isn't who I am. I don't scare easy, but this *pinche pendejo*, this thing, it frightens the shit out of me."

I believed her. I believed that she was really scared. But that wasn't enough.

We agreed to meet again.

"Thanks," she said, getting up. "You're a good person for doing this."

"I'll be in touch," I said.

She started walking to the door, but then stopped and took a few steps back toward me.

"You know, sometimes right after I see him, I don't feel myself. It's almost like he's—"

But she didn't finish. She just shook her head.

I swallowed hard and watched her go outside. She stopped at the sidewalk and looked down at the street for a long time, stroking her chin. Then she got into her car and drove away.

***

I had trouble sleeping that night.

Paloma Suárez seemed a little out there. I wasn't ready to buy into everything she was saying. But as I tossed and turned, I started thinking about the ghosts I had seen before. Some needed help. One even helped me. But I had never come in contact with a ghost like she was describing.

Staring up at the ceiling in the dark, I knew that if what this woman was saying was true and if I decided to try and help her, I might be in over my head.

I told myself that I was getting ahead of myself, that I still had a lot of fact finding to do before I crossed that river. After all, I had also felt like Annabelle and Spenser were "haunting" me when I first encountered them. But in the end, they just needed help. Maybe this was the same thing. Or maybe this Paloma Suárez just had a screw loose.

But my mind refused to listen to logic. It raced far ahead like a runaway stagecoach through the long sleep-less night.

Chapter 3

I got too far under the ball and watched as it sailed high, past the bright lights, and into the dark sky before bouncing out into the desert brush, nowhere near the goal.

I should have done more with it. We had only been down a goal and there were still a few minutes left in the game. The shot could have made the difference. At least I could have rolled it in on target. If I had done that, there was the chance the goalkeeper could have tripped or been hit by lightning.

The keeper took his time retrieving the ball and then kicked it far down field. I didn't get it back again and the ref blew the whistle and it was official. We didn't make the playoffs.

"Darn it all," Tim said.

I was using stronger language in my head.

His glasses were fogged up and sliding down his nose.

"It was a long shot anyway. We don't really belong in the playoffs," he said. "We basically suck."

I went over to the sidelines. Tim was right. It hadn't been a good season. I had barely practiced all summer and we only had won two games. It would have been a complete fluke to have advanced.

I didn't say much and grabbed my stuff, heading to the parking lot. I sat in the Jeep, drinking water while texting Kate that I was heading home.

I jumped at the knock on the window.

"Oh, sorry," Tim said as I rolled it down. "Uh, we're going out for drinks next week. Just wanted to invite you and let you know."

"Thanks. I'll be there."

"Hey, have a good night. And be careful out there."

I didn't know what he meant for a minute, but then remembered that he was just referring to my day job. We had talked a few times about me being a river guide and he told me that going on rivers freaked him out ever since he was a kid and had a bad experience. I didn't ask him what happened. I didn't want to start swapping drowning stories. But since finding out what I did during my days, Tim usually said goodbye with a worried expression and a reminder to be careful.

"I will," I said. "Goodnight."

It was a dark, moonless night. But down in the city it was bright. Bend had become popular over the last few years, maybe because of all the breweries in town. It was a record year for beer festivals. BrewFest, Fermentation Celebration, and The Little Woody all seemed to keep bringing more and more tourists in.

Ty was spending his weekend pouring at an event. He invited me to come along, but I passed. I was pretty tired and was looking forward to hanging out and watching some black and white movies and catching up on my sleep.

Yawning, I thought again about the soccer ball way up in the sky as I turned toward home.

***

The sound of a lone frog echoed in the darkness. I was sitting in the big Adirondack chair pushed up near the pond, staring at the dark silhouettes of the moving trees.

The air smelled heavy, like it was raining somewhere far away. But there wasn't a single cloud in the sky, just thousands of glittering stars in the darkness, reminding me of Ty.

He had been teaching me a little bit about the night sky this summer, showing me the details of the world above. I had never given it much thought before, but there was an entire universe up there, full of life and myths and stories and passion.

And sitting out here like this, when I thought about Ty, I usually also thought about Jesse.

It didn't make any sense that I loved them both. But that's how I felt. I couldn't help it.

I had seen Jesse only a couple of times during the summer. We walked through the park along the river and I told him about work and a little bit about my new friends. I asked him about what he did but he never said too much about where he was spending his time, just that he was somewhere else.

We rarely talked about Ty, but I was sure he knew about him. He had to.

Thinking about Jesse standing in the shadows of my life and watching me fall in love with someone else sent a wave of sadness through me.

I held the air in my lungs and then blew it out slowly.

"I'll always love you, Jesse," I whispered into the wind, hoping it would take the message to him.

Hoping that he would understand.

Chapter 4

"Really?" I said to Ty. "He really asked that?"

We were sitting outside on the upstairs deck, overlooking Bond Street, eating dinner at the Deschutes Brewery Pub. Cars rumbled below us and people walked, some stumbled, along the sidewalk.

"Yep," he said, smiling and wiping his mouth with a napkin. "It happened just like I said. The guy was from out of town and with a straight face, he asked me for a *butt* beer."

We both laughed again, my nose stinging from the Coke shooting up.

"He said it," Ty said. "Really. It's a direct quote. 'I'll have one of those black butt porters.'"

"So what did you tell him?" I said.

"I told him he'd have to go to Deschutes Brewery for the butt beer. That they made it, not us. The group he was with busted up and someone told him that the beer is called Black *Butte* Porter, not Butt Porter. The poor bastard turned all red."

Ty smiled in that way that sent chills through me and as I looked at him, those tingling feelings inside rose up in waves. He reached across the table and took my hand.

"Sorry I can't hang out with you tonight," he said. "I feel really bad about it."

We were supposed to be going out, but he had gotten called into work. He was learning about brewing and they were starting a new batch later.

"Don't feel bad. It's a great opportunity."

The waiter came over and put down the beer that Ty had ordered on the table.

"Okay," he said, nodding his head. "You've gotta try this. On tap it's totally different and I think you'll like it now."

I took a sip of the foaming liquid. He was right. It was a lot better than the bottled version. But I still liked the pale ales best.

"Not bad," I said.

He smiled as he stuffed the rest of his elk burger in his mouth. I finished the last of the sweet potato fries on my plate and drained my Coke.

"So all your groups on the river were all right today?" I asked. "I noticed some exuberant types with you there at the end."

"They weren't too bad," he said.

Ty never minded the rowdy teens and they usually wound up in his raft. He was pretty good with them and was able to keep the young punks in line.

"How about your groups?" he asked.

"They were all fine. Those ladies from the photography workshop in the last run were really nice. I got some serious tips from them, too."

"Money tips or photography tips?" he asked.

I held up my hand and rubbed my thumb and fingers together.

"That's what I'm talking about," he said.

I watched as a large group walked behind Ty and headed over to the empty table at the far end of the balcony. I recognized a few of them from soccer, players on some of the other teams. I waved when one of them looked over at me. He waved back.

"It's so busy in here tonight," I said. "I'm surprised we haven't bumped into any of our rafting customers."

"That's no coincidence. I always tell them to go over to Ten Barrel, that we have the better product. Which is true, you know."

I smiled.

"Then why are we here?"

"Research," he said.

I sat back.

"Oh, so Kate said she'll come to The Shins with us. She's writing a story on people who go to the concerts for free while they float on the river."

"Good," he said, smiling. "It's about time she gets in the canoe and does a Schwab concert right."

The river ran right by the outdoor venue and some people floated in watercrafts, listening to the concerts.

"What is she up to these days?" he asked.

"Working on some big story. She seems like her old self again."

I loved all the work Kate had done on the house, but I was glad when she started putting in extra hours at the newspaper again. Journalism was in her blood and it was where she belonged.

"I'll be right back," Ty said.

I stared out at the street. Some girls wearing bikini tops drove by and honked at a group of guys walking down the street. They whistled and started punching one another on the arm.

As I glanced over at the soccer players a few tables away, I noticed someone standing behind one of them. He was an older man, maybe a grandfather or uncle. He was smiling as he watched her eat.

I looked away quickly, even though there was nothing wrong, nothing that the old man ghost wanted from me. I saw these ghosts occasionally, but I always heard Jesse's voice in my head, telling me to focus on this world, not the ghost world.

Ty and I still didn't talk about it, and I wasn't sure how I felt about that. Sometimes I hated it because it felt like there was an elephant ghost in the room that nobody spoke about. And if something came up, like a problem, I knew that Ty wasn't the one I could go to for help.

But at other times, I kind of liked that he wasn't all that interested in ghosts. He was unusual that way. Most people had a strong opinion about it one way or another. And not talking about it was sometimes a good thing.

In some ways, Jesse would be happy about Ty. He would like that I found someone who could give me a normal kind of life.

Ty walked back, bringing his sunglasses down over his eyes.

"Sorry I have to get going, Abby. They just called. I guess they're starting earlier. I told them I was on my way. Actually, I think I'll just walk."

The waiter came with the check and Ty handed him his credit card.

He reached across the table and took my hand.

"I wish I could hang out with you longer," he said.

I stared at him and for a moment, it was only us. I wondered if that was what it was going to feel like when we were together. That we would be one and everything else would fall away except these feelings fluttering around.

"Me too," I said. "Next week though I want a real date. Dinner. Movie. The whole kit and caboodle."

"Wow," he said. "The whole kit and caboodle. I guess things are getting serious between us."

He smiled as the waiter came back, breaking our eye contact. Ty signed the receipt.

We walked down the stairs, past the small crowd waiting for seats, and outside. We lingered for another moment in front of the pub and then he kissed me goodbye.

"I love you, Abby," he whispered as his hand fell on my waist.

Those strong feelings moved fast around me, but again the words stuck hard in my throat. But he wasn't waiting for a response.

"Okay. I'll call you on my break. Have a good night."

"Okay. Bye."

I watched him walk away.

Chapter 5

"Hey Abby," Kate said. She was pouring hot water into a mug, the tea bag bouncing up and down.

"Hi," I said.

Her hair was pulled up in a loose bun on top of her head and she was wearing an old T-shirt that was splattered with paint, the one she always wore when she was fixing up the house.

"There can't be anything left to paint in here," I said as I passed by, staring at the stains on the shirt.

"No, the house is done," she said. "It's just comfortable."

I knew it was also Dr. Mortimer's. She had brought it home back one morning when they were dating. I wondered if she had gotten an email from him. He was still in India, working in a hospital.

"Want some tea? I just opened up a fresh Earl Grey."

I smiled, not sure if there was such a thing as fresh tea in a box.

"Sure," I said. "I'll be back in a few minutes."

I was tired, which meant there was a likely chance of sleeping through the night. I wasn't taking the sleeping pills anymore and most nights I was okay. It was good to be tired. It helped calm my thoughts. When I had something on my mind, I usually found myself outside staring up at the stars, waiting for dawn.

I took a quick shower and walked back out into the living room with wet hair. It was warm in the house. I found Kate on the sofa, watching one of those crime shows she loved. She was good at solving the cases and usually had it figured out after the first few minutes.

She handed me a cup and we watched the segment. It was about a husband who was suspected of murdering his wife even though no body had been found. They were trying to build the case on blood evidence and testimonials.

Kate muted the TV when it went to a commercial.

"So how was your day?" she asked, folding her legs and turning toward me.

"It was fine. Easy runs, friendly people. And no one fell in."

It was a lame attempt at a joke, but when I saw Kate's face fall for a minute I wished I hadn't said it. She was still uncomfortable about me being a river guide and sometimes I forgot that it was best not to give her too many details about my day.

She sighed, but then forced a smile.

I took a sip of tea. It was just how I liked it, not too strong with a little cream.

"Were you able to get ahold of that guy today?"

She nodded.

"You bet I did. It wasn't easy. He was avoiding me, so I finally just drove over there and waited outside his office."

I cringed. Since the bombing, I had a new perspective on reporters.

Kate picked up on my thoughts right away.

"This guy's a predator, Abby. It's not at all like your situation. And he's a public employee. He works for the city. He doesn't get to hide."

"So how long did you have to wait for him?"

"About twenty minutes. He was trying to sneak out the back door, but I caught up to him. I threatened to run the story with what I had, which wasn't going to be flattering. He talked, denying it. So at least I have a few quotes from him now."

It was nice seeing the old spark back in Kate's eyes as she talked about her job. Writing stories like this one was what she lived for.

"Excellent," I said.

Our lives had really gotten back to normal.

The only thing that wasn't like before was that Dr. Mortimer was still gone. I didn't know what Kate was going to do. I had the sense she was still waiting, still hoping that he would sort things out and make his way back to her. But it was hard to ignore that he seemed to be building a life for himself in India. And I knew that it must hurt, although she didn't talk about it much.

"Is Ty working tonight?"

"Yeah, every night this week," I said. "I barely see him anymore."

She laughed.

"Well, except all day on the river. You two seem good together. Happy."

"Yeah," I said. "We are."

"That's great," she said, smiling.

She unmuted the TV. The agents were off to arrest the husband.

I got up.

"Ouch!" she said. "That's gotta hurt."

"It does," I said, holding my breath until the pain passed. "That's the one thing I hate about leather sofas. Summer."

I took the cups into the kitchen.

"Well, it's late. I think I'll head to bed," Kate said when I came back. "Oh, I found an article today on how to buy tickets to the soccer games in Barcelona. I sent you an email."

I had been saving for my Barcelona trip, and the extra hours I worked all summer were helping me to believe that I was actually going to go. Plus I had a little money that our mom had left me.

"Cool," I said. "I'll read it tonight. I hope you can come too, Kate. When was the last time we went on a real vacation?"

"It's been too long. I might be able to make it happen. We'll see."

I said goodnight and stepped out in the backyard, watching the trees and listening to the frogs.

Chapter 6

I turned the sign over and pulled down the blinds. I collected the unopened sugar packets that had been left on the counter and put them back in the little ceramic container.

David put down the stack of money he was counting.

"Really, Abby Craig, in my own defense, Paloma Suárez looks a lot different than when she came in here that day. I mean *a lot* different."

I was long over his temporary bout of amnesia, but I was still giving him a hard time. David had told me where Paloma worked. I had never been to Club 6 before.

"Really?" I said.

"Oh, yeah. At the club she wears a lot more makeup and little outfits with lots of shimmer and sparkle to spare. It's like Chris Isaak designs her threads. You know, dancers have to look hot."

"She's a dancer? I thought she was a bartender."

David smiled.

"She dances in the cage most of the time, tends bar the rest of the time."

"The cage?"

"Yeah," he said, looking up. "Club 6 has this cage that hangs down from the ceiling and people get in it and dance, dance, dance. Eddie likes the girls at the bar to get up in there so the customers will buy more drinks from them."

"Sounds like quite the place," I said.

"It is. It's a little east of seedy, but who doesn't need that once in a while, right?"

I smiled and shrugged.

He finished counting out the register and then went in the back for a few minutes while I put the last of the canisters away.

"Anyway, we're all good now," he said, grabbing his stuff from behind the counter. "I saw her just last night."

We turned out the lights and walked outside. I stood in the warm air as he locked the front door.

"So, are you helping her or what? I mean, she seems really freaked out still. She told me it's worse than ever. I guess she's talking about the ghost bugging her."

"Yeah," I said. "I'm going to try. I'm meeting her tomorrow morning."

We walked over to our cars, which were parked close to each other out on the street.

"You going to The Shins tomorrow night?" he asked.

"Well, yeah, sort of," I said. "We'll be in a canoe."

He sighed and rolled his eyes.

"Now that sounds like one hot date with Mr. Big Spender," he said. "What's the encore? Feeding geese in the park at midnight?"

"Ha, ha, ha," I said.

"Anyway, I'll be there. We actually bought tickets, so I get to sit on the grass and watch the band and everything. But maybe I'll go over to the river and search for you guys and say hi. If I can't find you, just shoot off a flare or something."

I smiled.

"I'll be there with some of those friends you met when we went out for your birthday that night."

"That was fun," I said. "Your friends are a blast."

It was a really good night. It was at the beginning of the summer and Ty and I had met up with David for a night of bar hopping to celebrate my 21st birthday.

"I guess we're kind of lucky that we saw Mo play that night," David said, standing in the street with the door open. "Now that she's a big star and everything. Who knows if she'll even come back to Bend? Maybe it's straight to Hollywood."

I unlocked my Jeep.

"Maybe," I said, thinking Mo would be the last person to go Hollywood.

"Well, good night, Abby Craig."

"Good night, David Norton."

As I drove home I thought about Mo and her band. They were really pretty good. The lead singer had this low, sultry voice and it mixed well with the driving rock sound they were putting out. Mo was great on her guitar solos and I could tell that she really loved being up on stage, lost in the riffs. That it was what she was born to do.

I thought back to her brother. His ghost had helped us stop the school bombing.

"It feels better knowing what really happened to him," Mo had said to me the day before she left. "You know, I always felt bad about him, how it happened. Like it was my fault. But now that I know the whole story, it doesn't hurt so much."

It was a good thing, being at peace, and I was glad that I had helped her.

I turned up my street, thinking that maybe there was someone else I could be helping, too.

Chapter 7

There were a few other runners making their way around the college track.

It felt too early to be here. But here I was just the same. It was 7:08. I was sluggish, slower than a snail on gravel, my legs refusing to move any faster as I pushed them to the length of the three miles I had promised myself I'd do.

"Come on," I said out loud near the finish.

It was only the first day of my new early morning routine. Maybe it would get easier. I couldn't imagine it getting any harder. I was determined to build my endurance and work on my speed. The new soccer season wasn't that far away and I was going to be ready this time, no matter how many hours I worked.

By the time I stumbled across the finish line, the sun was above the horizon, hot in my face. Sweat burned my eyes.

I sucked air for the next few minutes, walking for a while and then stretching.

Afterwards I looked around for Paloma Suárez. We had agreed to meet at eight.

"Hey, Abby," she said, coming up behind me.

I turned and saw bags under her bloodshot eyes, a fast gray energy moving quickly around her.

"So you do this every day?" she said.

"Oh, hi. Well, that's the plan. We'll have to see how long I can stand it."

"You're a better man than me," she said. "*Híjole.* I wouldn't do it, even if they paid me."

We walked over to a table near the school's library.

"Are things any better?" I asked, sensing the answer before she spoke.

"No," she said. "Worse."

"It's been my experience that they usually want something. Maybe help. Do you have a feeling about what he might want?"

She let out a long breath and looked at the tall trees surrounding the track.

"Me," she said finally. "He wants me."

"Why do you think that?"

"I know that sounds crazy," she said. "Maybe I'm just being dramatic. I don't know, maybe it's all in my head. If nothing else, Abby, I'm hoping you settle that. If it's just me being crazy or not. Because the people I talk to, that's what they all think. That I've gone off the deep end."

"I'll do what I can," I said, not sure what that might be.

"Can you just stop by the club and see if you see him? I've asked the bouncer, the customers, even the owner. This creepy guy is standing not ten feet away, and I'm the only one who can see him. If you came by, maybe you can tell me what you see."

"Yeah, I can do that. No problem."

"Thanks, Abby. I can't tell you how much that means. You know, I even asked my sister to come in this last weekend. That shows how desperate I am. She doesn't want me working at the club. I don't know how many fights we've had over it. But she didn't see him either. She's a nurse over at the hospital, so her first thought was that I need to see a counselor or something. She thinks I'm mental. And the worst thing is that she might be right."

I nodded slowly, remembering that feeling, how everyone thought I was a freak after my accident because I said I still saw Jesse. Even though he was dead. And I sure knew how it felt to have a sister who disapproved of my job. Kate had made progress, but she was still uncomfortable with me working on the river. Not that I could blame her. After all, I had drowned.

It didn't mean that Paloma was really being haunted, but it did make me want to help her.

"So David tells me you're a dancer?" I said.

She shook her head.

"Oh, so David remembers me now? How lucid of him. Yeah, they hired me as a bartender last year, but when business slowed down in the winter they cut my position. Eddie, the owner, said I could stay on as a cage dancer. At first I thought, no way, *pinche buey*, but with the economy the way it is, I didn't feel like I could say no. He still lets me mix drinks when we get busy. Plus, it's not like I'm a stripper or nothing. I'm not wearing much, but my vital organs are covered."

"Well, if there's a real ghost hanging around the club, I think I'll be able to see him," I said. "I can stop by in the next few days."

"That would be awesome."

"Has he done anything to you?" I said.

"No. I guess not. So far he just stares."

My legs were tightening up.

"Do you mind if we walk a little?" I said.

"Let's do it."

We headed back to the track and started walking on the two outside lanes.

"So when did it all start?" I asked, putting on my sunglasses.

"I started seeing him about a month ago. Just once in a while at first. In the corner or on the other side of the dance floor. Or up against a wall in the back of the club. He would just stand there and look at me, and then he disappeared. Like I said, at first I thought he was a customer, although now that I think back on it he never did order anything."

"Then what?"

"Then he started hanging around more. And he moved in closer. Last week, he was standing right at the bar, next to the last seat. Leering, full of... hate, I guess. I finally asked the bouncer to toss him, but of course he didn't know what I was talking about."

I felt a sudden cold creep down my back.

"One night last week, I couldn't take it anymore. I decided to go up to him myself and tell him to leave. I wasn't going to put up with it all night again, him staring at me like that. Like he wanted to do terrible things. I walked right up to him and told him."

"What did he do?"

"He just grinned at me," she said. "His eyes looked right into me for a moment and then he just disappeared there in front of me. Faded. It was like some magic trick. I've been drinking lately just to get through my shift, maybe drinking more than I should. During the day I think that maybe that accounts for it. But when I see him I feel shaky and sober at the same time. And I know he's real."

"What does he look like?" I asked.

"Well, he's kind of stocky. Not too tall. But he has this strong, big chest. I'd say he's in his 40's and has dark features. Dirty black hair hanging down over his forehead. And a mustache."

I suddenly had an uncontrollable urge to look around and make sure no one fitting that description was nearby.

"But the strangest thing about him are his eyes," Paloma said. "They're striking. The kind of eyes you never forget. They're light blue and super bright. That was the first thing that I noticed about him. And when I looked into his eyes the last time I saw him, it felt as if I got stuck in quicksand. Like I was caught. Trapped. It was really horrible."

She started crying.

"When I finally broke free from him, from those eyes, I knew. I knew he was..."

She hesitated.

"What? What did you know?"

Her eyes went wide with terror.

"That he was really bad. No, not bad. Evil. That I was staring right into evil."

She stopped in her tracks for a moment like she had lost all her strength from telling me the story.

"Sorry," she said. "I'm just exhausted. I... haven't... I barely sleep anymore. I just dread the entire day because I have to go back there."

"You only see him when you're at the club?"

"I look for him everywhere I go. I'm paranoid I might see him at the store or at the gym. I walk around with sharp rocks in my gut. I can't even eat anymore. But so far, yeah, just at the club."

I sighed.

"Can you take a little time off work?"

"Eddie isn't too big on time off. I would quit if I could afford it. And I'm afraid that if I leave I might have trouble finding another job anytime soon."

Maybe her paranoia was contagious, but I suddenly felt his dark energy all around. I shuddered.

"So you see a lot of ghosts?" she asked.

"A few. But the ghosts I've seen and interacted with haven't been like what you're describing. But I'll come and take a look. Maybe there's more to the story. Maybe I can help you figure out why he's hanging around."

"Thanks again, Abby," she said. She hesitated before giving me a hug.

"See you at the club," I said. "I'll call you to confirm."

She smiled and nodded and started walking away up the hill to the parking lot.

"Do you have a boyfriend?" she asked, turning back around.

"Yeah," I said.

"Bring him."

Chapter 8

Ty stood over me as I gasped, stunned by the cold water. I held tight to the paddleboard while I tried to catch my breath.

"Damn!" I said, bobbing in the river.

Crawling back on top of the board was easy enough, but I had trouble standing up again. I was on my knees, the board wobbling under me as the current carried me downriver. I was about to tumble in one more time.

"You're okay," Ty said. "Just take a breath and balance yourself before you try and stand. Take your time. You'll get it."

I extended my legs, threw my butt high in the air and jerked up with absolutely no grace whatsoever.

"Sweet!" he yelled. "Good work."

I was using his roommate's paddleboard and we were on the Deschutes, in front of the Old Mill.

We headed back up river, side by side, to the park. It was a good arm workout going against the current, especially under the bridge where the water was strong. We carried our boards to his truck and slid them in.

"Do you have a few minutes to sit in the sun so I could dry off?" I asked.

We both had to get to work, but I was feeling happy and lazy and didn't want to leave. We walked over to the grass and he pulled me down and then on top of him, laughing.

I laughed too.

"Well, not too bad for your first time," he said.

I smiled, staring into his eyes, and sat up.

"Your technique got better and better as time went on," he said. "You had more confidence on that last stretch. You did great."

"Well, thanks. I did fall in, though."

"That's just part of learning. I've fallen in a thousand times."

"Okay, if you say so," I said. "It was pretty fun. Sign me up for another lesson."

"You're on. So you practicing after work today?" he said.

"Yep," I said. "I have a game tomorrow night."

"I want to come running with you sometime," he said. "And as you know, I'm always available to be your goalie."

I laughed. Ty was really bad, but I liked playing with him.

"Come on, I can't get better if I don't get out there, right? I'm not like you. I was on horses when I was a kid, not soccer fields."

"I know," I said, pretending to play a violin. "Poor deprived Ty guy."

We both laughed before I took off running toward the parking lot, his footsteps right behind me.

Chapter 9

It had been a hard, hot, long day.

Hard because of the constant flow of tourists and locals streaming through the doors. Hot because we were in the third day of a sweltering heat wave with the temperatures over 100 degrees. And long because the air conditioner still wasn't fixed, causing a slew of complaints from angry customers.

"It feels like hell in here," said a plump, middle-aged regular. She wiped off her forehead with the back of her hand, her gold bracelets clanking together. "I mean, really. This is ridiculous. It's been days. Has Mike hired someone or is he trying to just fix it himself?"

I nodded. Smiled. Waited.

"Tell him that I like it here, but Thump has good coffee, too. Not to mention Starbucks. And I'm sure that they have their air working."

I replied with a technique I had found most successful when dealing with difficult customers.

"You're right," I said. "What can I get started for you?"

She gave me a sour look but went ahead and ordered her usual non-fat latte.

"Iced," she added and rolled her eyes as she moved over to the machines.

"Bet you're wishing you were on the river with Ty Terrifico instead of working here at Satan's Left Armpit," David said under his breath as he passed by.

I smiled. He was right. I would take a set of angry rapids any day over a set of angry customers.

I helped the next two women, who were actually happy and friendly and didn't seem upset at all with the heat. They both ordered and left tips and walked down to the end of the bar.

After a little while, I took my break and wandered over to the back room, where it was cooler and darker, the air loaded with the rich smell of coffee beans. I could hear the workers pounding away. Maybe they would get it fixed sometime today.

I walked over to the sink and washed my face and then looked at myself in the mirror. I had a pretty good tan going, but a few freckles were now sprinkled across my cheeks.

"Abby Craig," David said, singing my name as he walked up to me. He was carrying a tray of dirty mugs to the dishwasher. "So when do you get out of here?"

"I'm closing," I said.

"Ugh," David said. "That's a bummer."

"You?" I asked.

"One more hour. Mike asked if I could stay on, but I said no way. This heat is making me sick. Maybe Mike should just shut us down till it's fixed. Aren't there laws or something about making people work in these conditions?"

David was a big baby sometimes, but he wasn't wrong. It was too hot and I was also wondering the same thing, although not about the laws, just about whether we would close or not.

I caught David in the mirror staring at me, a strange expression on his face.

"Sorry again about the Paloma thing," he said.

"It would be nice to be able to talk to you about this sort of stuff. I wish I had a friend I could trust that way. I don't really even talk to Ty about it."

"I promise to do better," he said, sounding sincere. "I will. I want you to tell me everything about the ghosts you see. I think it's fascinating. That's why I blab. But no more. I will zip it."

When I looked at him, I was surprised to see that he wasn't smiling. It was one of the few times I had ever seen him so serious.

"Well, good," I said.

He came a little closer.

"Okay, I'm just going to come clean," he said. "I told my mom about you, this was a long time ago, promise. Like back when you were dealing with that Kaboom High School thing. Anyway, she wanted me to ask. We were wondering if you see any of my dead relatives around me. You know, like their ghosts."

I paused for a moment, looking at him.

"You told your mom about me?"

"Well, it just sort of came out," he said, smiling. "She read about you in her newspaper and I was all like, I work with that girl. I was proud, Abby Craig. That's all."

I scrunched the paper towel into a ball and threw it at his head, but it bounced off his shoulder when he ducked.

"What?" he said, laughing. "She watches a lot of those ghost shows and she was so excited when I told her. She's hoping you can see my Aunt Jenny or my grandma or somebody else. So, do you see anyone?"

He closed his eyes as if summoning spirits.

"All right," I said. "Let's see."

I had never seen any ghosts around David, but I looked at him quietly now anyway. His white and gray energy moved in faster waves around him, telling me that he was both excited and nervous about what I might find. Just to make sure he thought I was being thorough, I took my time.

"No," I said. "Sorry, but nobody's there."

He looked a little disappointed when he opened his eyes.

"Really, David," I said. "It's a good thing. Some of the ghosts I see are pretty scary."

He smiled.

"Oh, okay. If you say so. I guess I was just hoping. I mean, I really miss my grandma. So just let me know if you see something."

"I will," I said. "Promise. But only if you can keep it a secret. Things have finally gotten back to normal and I like it that way."

"Deal," he said. "Sorry again. And I'm glad those brutal newspaper people are leaving you alone."

"Me too," I said, sighing. "I better enjoy it while it lasts."

David gave me a quick look, trying to figure out what I meant. I was thinking about the trial scheduled for December and all the publicity that would be involved. David still didn't know anything about Nathaniel Mortimer or the other scientists who had tried to kill me.

"You cooking up some other ghost story for the press or something?" he asked.

"No, nothing like that," I said. "But Kate always says once in the public eye, always in the public eye."

"Hmmm," he said. "Okay then. Well, I guess we better get back out there before Mike throws a fit."

We walked up to the front and he groaned as we stared at the line wrapped around the tables and over to the bathrooms in the back of the store.

Chapter 10

It was just after the first small set of rapids when they started in.

"Don't worry, sweetheart," the gray-haired man sitting closest to me said. "If we capsize I'll save you."

"Don't trust him, hon," another one said. "Alone with him in the water? It would be a disaster!"

They all broke out in laughter.

There were seven of them in my raft, middle-aged, all wearing the same hats and shirts, some with the price tag still hanging off the back.

"Hey, sugar, let's pick it up a little and make this a *real* ride," yelled the guy up front, turning completely around so that I could hear him.

I put my personal feelings and wishes aside. After two seasons of guiding, I hadn't had one customer fall into the water. I didn't want to start with these idiots.

I was ready for a little break and happy to make it on shore to scout the upcoming rapids. I smiled when I saw Ty waiting. He helped steady the raft while everybody got out and started walking down the short trail.

"Hey, sweetheart, wanna switch groups?" Ty said in a low voice after the men were out of earshot.

We rarely switched, but we all had an understanding that sometimes certain people were better with certain guides and that it really was in everybody's best interest to feel comfortable going down the rapids.

"No," I said. "I'm okay. They're not that bad. Just 52 cards short of a full deck, if you know what I mean."

"And you're just left with the jokers, huh?"

"Exactly."

He squeezed my hand before letting go. I was hoping he would stay here with me and the rafts and let one of the other guides talk to the group, but he started following them to the rocks.

"Have fun," I said.

As he caught up with them, they swarmed around him, full of questions. He was all smiles and charm as usual. I stayed back on shore with Amber and Pam, sitting in the shade after we made sure the boats were tied down. It was another scorching day and that sweet smell of pine needles filled the air, lingering as we talked about our plans for after the season.

Amber was going back to her job at a bakery. Pam was going to work in a physical therapy office. Neither of them seemed too thrilled.

"So what about you, Abby?"

"I'll probably just pick up more hours at Back Street for a while," I said. "Maybe something else. I'm not sure."

They nodded and Pam sighed.

"It's so nice out here," she said. "I'm sure going to miss it."

I felt better after sitting there for a few minutes at the edge of the forest, remembering how lucky I was that I was able to run the river all summer. It was a good life.

"So how are things going with Ty?" Amber asked as she rolled up the sleeves on her T-shirt.

"No complaints," I said.

"You guys seem really great together," Pam said. "But in case you didn't know, it's making the front office girls crazy."

I did know actually. Neither of them said goodbye to me anymore when I checked out.

"But us guides are all really, really happy for you two," Amber said.

The tourists were heading back over toward us and we got up and untethered the boats. We got in and pushed off. I back paddled while we waited for Ty's raft to go first. I usually followed him down the rapids, staying in his wake.

My fools were a little quieter and listened as I reminded them about their footing and about paddling. It was how it usually was when we were heading into the deafening roar of the whitewater, when the waves started pushing us around. It tended to separate the men from the boys. And the sweethearts.

"Paddle left!" I shouted.

They followed directions like it was a team-building exercise. We were headed into a giant boulder, but I wasn't too worried. We had time and I steered us into a good position, shooting around it and then letting the river take us down, throwing us into the sudden calm waters at the end of the run.

"Amazing!" one of them yelled.

As the men climbed onto the bus later, one of them walked over and handed me two twenties, the biggest tip I'd ever gotten.

"Thanks, that was really fun," he said.

"Glad to hear it," I said, pocketing the cash.

I looked over at Ty. He started laughing.

"So, sweetie, does this mean you're buying dinner tonight?" he said.

I punched him in the arm and we grabbed the paddles and life vests and walked up to the shuttle bus.

Chapter 11

I circled the park. It was still hot. Large cauliflower clouds drifted across the sky up above. The weatherman had been talking about storms for days, but so far nothing had materialized.

I walked past the basketball court and watched the game for a minute. It was three on three and both teams were making most of their shots. Just as I thought of him, I glanced over at the bench and saw someone sitting, wearing a baseball cap.

"Jesse," I said, walking up to him, my heart fluttering.

"Hey," he said, adjusting his hat. He stood up and gave me a long hug.

"You're looking good, Craigers. Tan, lean, happy. I'd say you're almost glowing even."

He smiled like there was something hidden in the words.

"You too," I said, as we sat back down. "Except for the tan part."

He looked at his arms.

"Man, I try. But so far, no luck."

His eyes wandered back to the game.

"These guys are good," he said. "You should watch them and get some pointers."

"You're better," I said.

"Yeah. But you could learn something when I'm not around."

I laughed, but then stopped suddenly as I wondered if there was some meaning in those words too.

That's how it was lately when I saw him. I always feared he was coming to tell me that he had to leave, that he was permanently going to that other world where he really belonged and we could no longer see each other. I sensed that it could happen at any time and I dreaded it.

I let the silence sit for a minute in case he wanted to add anything, but he was quiet.

"Relax, Craigers," he said, seeming to notice my tension. "I just dropped by to say hi. No big deal."

"Good," I said.

"See that guy with the Duncan jersey? Watch his wrist right before he releases the ball. That's what you need to work on. That flick. You shoot the ball like a professional brick layer. Work on that and you might not miss all your shots."

"I don't miss *all* my shots," I said, kicking him.

"So how's life? What are you up to?"

I told him a few stories about my days on the river. Then about David and how Kate was back at the newspaper, working a lot of hours.

"Whoa, did you see that?"

The guy had just nailed a three-pointer.

Jesse played with his hat again. He was trying hard to act normal, but I could tell there was something off about him, something on his mind.

"Let's walk," he said.

We strolled next to the river. I took his hand. It felt right holding it, but it was also confusing. The only hand I had been holding lately was Ty's. I didn't know what it meant.

"So you happy, Craigers?"

"Yeah. It's been a good stretch."

We stopped and watched a family of ducks float by. He was making me nervous again, saying things without saying them. We hadn't ever talked seriously about Ty, but I was pretty sure that's what he was getting at. Unless it was something else.

"Are you here to warn me about something?" I asked suddenly.

"Yeah, there might be thunder and lightning tonight followed by periods of darkness. Otherwise, no, no serious warnings today. But I want you to know that if something happens, I'll always be with you in one way or another. Even if you might not be able to see me."

"What do you mean?"

"I'm saying that it was foolish of me to tell you I would make sure to say goodbye if I had to leave. We don't know if that's possible. I couldn't find you the other morning. I was looking, but couldn't find your energy. It was blocked."

"Blocked?"

"That's not the right word. I don't know. I just couldn't find you."

"Really?" I said, trying to keep the panic out of my voice.

"It's something to know," he said. "That it might not always be a choice, me coming back to say goodbye."

"Okay," I said feeling deflated.

He turned and looked at me, his face serious. I stared up into those flecked eyes I loved so much.

"I'm glad you've had such a great summer," he said. "That's everything I wanted. For you to get your life back. And you have."

He turned and looked back at the river flowing gently past us, quiet for a moment.

"Remember that game you played in, the one where you scored all those goals against that Portland team who thought they were all that?"

I smiled.

"I'll never forget that game. It was my first and only hat trick."

"That was a hell of a thing."

I smiled and squeezed his hand.

"Those were the days," he said, sighing.

"The best."

He let go of my hand and I reached up and hugged him again.

"Well, bye, Craigers."

Tears fell from my eyes as I watched him disappear into the trees.

"I love you, Jesse," I said. "I'll always love you."

I didn't know if he could hear me.

Chapter 12

When I told Kate that Ty and I were heading out later to Club 6, she stopped and stared at me for a moment.

"Why on earth would you guys go there?" she said.

"That's where Paloma works," I said, taking my plate into the kitchen. "I told her I would drop by and say hello."

"Paloma?"

I had already told Kate about her a few days ago.

"Oh, yeah," she said. "She's the one with the ghost. I remember now. You didn't tell me she worked at that club. Can't you guys meet somewhere else?"

"No. That's where she says the ghost appears."

I could tell that she didn't want me to go, but she didn't say anything. I put on my sandals as she closed her laptop and stuffed it in her bag.

"Well, that's too bad she has to work there. Yuck."

"Have you ever been there?" I said.

"Oh, sure, years ago during my first few years of growing pains," she said. "But not since then. It's gotten worse too, from what everyone says. And they get a lot of police calls every weekend. Fights, drugs, that sort of thing. That place is bad news."

I nodded.

"We're meeting up with David."

"No surprise there," she said, smiling and grabbing her keys off the counter. "Bye, Abby. Have a good day out on the river. I'll be in Redmond covering a story all afternoon, but I'll call and check in when I can."

I said goodbye and finished the last bit of strong coffee at the kitchen sink. I stared out the window at the pond and the waterfall, wishing I had a little bit more time to linger and enjoy the morning.

***

Kate was right. Club 6 was pretty sketchy.

"We don't have to stay long," I shouted into Ty's ear over the pulsating dance music.

"Okay," he said, taking my hand and leading me toward the bar.

It was crowded and hot in the club, the smell of beer and sweat and smoke floating around, the beat of the music rumbling through my body. We walked past a group of guys arguing.

There was a dance floor in the middle of the large room, filled with people, some just talking, others throwing their bodies into one another. High in the air, hanging from the ceiling in the far corner was the large cage that David had described.

Someone was in it. For a moment I thought it might be Paloma but then noticed the dancer had long hair that she started whipping from side to side to the beat of the music.

I texted David to meet us at the bar. Supposedly he was here, somewhere in this gyrating, unwashed crowd.

We walked past girls in short skirts, the lights from the disco ball moving across their faces. Just as we got to the bar I turned and saw David on the floor, waving. He kept his hand high in the air as he danced over to us.

"Abby Craig!" he said, throwing both arms around me.

"Hi, David," I said, smiling.

"And Ty is here, too!" he said, giving him his own hug.

"Hey," Ty said, looking at me.

"I didn't know *you* were coming tonight too. I thought you were busy concocting vodka or whiskey or something. Yea, us! We're all here together!"

"It's crazy in here," I said.

"It's always like this," David said. "That's why it's so fun. Most of the clubs in this little town are dead, dead, dead. But not here. You do have to wait till after 11. You guys got here at the perfect time. Come on. First round's on me."

Paloma was at the far end of the bar, stacking glasses.

I hadn't told Ty the real reason I wanted to stop by Club 6, just that we were meeting David for a drink. I would tell him about Paloma and her problem eventually, but I figured I might as well make sure there really was a ghost before we had that talk.

"What'll it be?" David asked us, his eyes glazed and happy.

"I'll just take a Mirror Pond," Ty said.

"Me, too."

"You two grab those seats and I'll go order and tell her you're here."

We slid onto the stools, sitting next to a group watching boxing on the television above the bar. I scanned the crowd, looking for the ghost, but didn't see anyone who fit the description that Paloma had given me.

Behind the bar was the typical long mirror and shelves filled with glasses and bottles. Another bartender was working with Paloma, shaking a mixer and singing along to the music.

"Thanks for coming," I said to Ty.

"Of course."

Paloma waved when she saw me and then grabbed two beers. She opened them as she walked over and put them down in front of us.

"Hey, Abby!" she said. "Thanks for being here. It means a lot."

Ty tilted his head at me, like a dog trying to understand human speech.

"Paloma, this is my boyfriend," I said. "Ty."

She smiled and said hello, shaking his hand across the bar.

Like she had said, she wasn't wearing much. Mostly strings tied to other strings.

"Drinks are on David," she said. "He told me to tell you he'd catch up with you guys after this song. Anyway, enjoy. Let me know when you need another."

We sat and sipped our beers.

"To a great season," he said, raising his bottle.

I picked mine up and we toasted, the glass clinking together loudly.

"Indeed," I said, taking a big gulp.

The music seemed even louder than before as I scanned the dance floor for David, but he was lost in a sea of people. It was hot in the club and I felt for a moment like I was back at Back Street.

I studied the crowd. I didn't see the ghost dancing, didn't see him at the bar, or around Paloma.

"I'll be right back," I said. "Save my seat if you can."

I walked to the back. People were standing in line waiting to use the bathroom. There was a door that read "Staff Only."

When I came back out, I saw Paloma watching me as she made a drink. Her eyes were dancing to their own nervous music.

I weaved through the crowd, looking for the ghost. People were slouching against the wall and sitting at the bar. I looked over at the tables and at the different clusters standing around and drinking and talking.

But I didn't see him.

I went back over to the bar, squeezing between two girls who gave me dirty looks.

"Over there," Paloma said suddenly. "Do you see him?"

She pointed to a spot not far from where I was standing.

"There," she said. "Abby. Please tell me you see him. He's right there, staring at me."

I couldn't see anything.

"Sorry, Paloma. But I don't see him. Does he look the same, like you described the other day?"

"Yes," she said, her voice high. "Damn it, he's right there."

"I'll keep looking," I said.

"I'm on next," she said, throwing down her bar rag and heading toward the cage.

I felt for her, but I had to be honest. There was no ghost. None that I could see anyway.

I made my way back to Ty.

"So what's going on, Abby?" he asked.

"I'll tell you everything when we get out of here," I said.

I took another sip and looked around once more. David wasn't anywhere to be found and neither was the ghost.

Paloma was up in the cage. The original Beatles version of *Helter Skelter* was playing, the lights in the club flashing to the music.

We watched her for a little while.

"Your friend's got some moves," Ty said.

"And a lot of guts," I said.

It was time to go.

Suddenly an animal-like wail cut through the music and bounced off the walls. It had come from the direction of the cage. I looked up and saw Paloma hanging onto the bars and screaming.

"Get away from me, *Cucuy*! Get me out of here! Bring me down! Bring me down!"

I think most people didn't even hear her, or if they did they probably thought it was part of her act. But the bouncer made his way over and lowered the cage. Paloma slammed the door into him and took off into the back of the club.

I looked for her, checking the bathroom and dressing room, but she was gone.

***

Later as we walked along Bond, I told Ty the real reason we had been there, about how Paloma had come to Back Street looking for me and said she thought she was being haunted by a ghost.

He didn't say much. He took my hand and we walked quietly for a moment, heading back to his truck.

"I wish you had told me," he said. "You know, before we went. I know I haven't always been understanding about that stuff. But I just wish you would have told me."

I nodded.

"I'll work on it," I said.

He didn't like to hear about my ability or gift or whatever it was. Every time I talked about ghosts or visions, he froze up without saying too much, leaving me feeling like I used to a long time ago.

"It's just that it was easier," I said. "To find out about it first. I didn't even see a ghost in there tonight. So what would have been the point of that conversation?"

He shook his head.

"The point would have been honesty."

We got into his truck. He was quiet on the drive home. He didn't seem angry exactly, more like disappointed. We pulled up to the house and he left the engine running.

"Bye," I said.

He sighed.

"Just tell me the truth next time, Abby. I can handle it."

"Okay," I said. "I will."

He gave me a hollow kiss and drove off.

Chapter 13

It was the nightmare that woke me.

I was submerged in cold water, holding my breath, refusing to take it into my lungs while they all watched me from above.

Waiting.

Waiting for me to die.

My eyes flew open and I gasped for air, staring at the bright glow from the television lighting up the living room. I was on the sofa, my head on a cushion with a blanket over me. The end of *Casablanca* was playing. It was the final scene, the part where Bogart watches the woman he loves get on an airplane with another man and fly away forever.

I turned it off after he and Claude Rains walked off together.

"Just a dream," I said to my reflection in the bathroom.

Most nights I was sleeping better. Most nights I made it through without waking up and didn't have those kinds of dreams. Maybe it was the club, or Ty. Or maybe I had been thinking too much about Paloma before falling asleep, wondering if she really was crazy.

I washed my face and walked back out. I grabbed the fleece blanket and wrapped it around my shoulders, turned off the security alarm, and stepped outside.

It was a beautiful night. Cool and breezy. I sat down by the pond and listened to the water.

It hadn't felt like a lie, not really. But Ty was right that I shouldn't have been so secretive about why I wanted to go to the club. I didn't like keeping things from him, but the truth was I was never sure if he could handle my ghost sightings. I rarely told him much about the other world I saw sometimes. It was just easier to not talk about it.

Until something happened, like tonight, that reminded us that there were things in our relationship that still needed work. Would I ever feel comfortable talking about ghosts with him? Would he ever be able to handle it?

But when I thought about him on the river and how his eyes looked in the sunlight when he was standing by the rafts and laughing, I felt better about us.

The kitchen light went on and Kate poked her head out the door and then headed over.

"You okay?"

"Yeah. Just a little trouble sleeping, no big deal."

"Me too," she said, sitting down and yawning.

We sat listening to the water falling gently over the rocks in the pond.

"So you survived?" she asked. "How was it?"

"It was all right," I said. "I didn't see a ghost or anything."

"That's good, I suppose."

"Yeah, it was kind of weird."

I told her about Paloma freaking out and about how I was wondering if she was crazy. I also mentioned some of the Ty stuff.

"You guys will figure it out. Every relationship has its baggage."

"A small carry-on would be fine. I just don't want it to turn into one of those refrigerator boxes held together with duct tape you see going around and around on the carousel at the airport."

"Yeah. Speaking of, I got an email from Ben earlier," she said.

"Anything new?"

"Not really. He seems better. He sent a picture of himself standing in front of the hospital where he's working. I forwarded it to you."

She looked over at me and then sighed, letting her head rest against the back of the chair.

"So, how long will you wait for him?"

"I don't think I'm waiting anymore," she said. "I love him, but that's just not going to be enough for this relationship."

It made me sad hearing it, but it was probably a good move. He seemed to be starting over somewhere else, with different people.

"But I'm better about it now," she said. "No worries. It's nice to be back at work. I've missed it."

"You seem good, Kate," I said because it was true and because maybe she needed to hear it.

"Yeah, I kinda feel like my old self lately," she said. "Well, I better start getting ready for work."

"Really?" I said. "What time is it?"

The darkness was fading, but it still had to be early.

"Almost five," she said. "I have an interview at seven and need to prepare."

I followed her inside, leaving the peace of the pond behind.

Chapter 14

After the third run of the day, something changed.

Dark clouds had blown in from the mountains. The hail and thunderstorm alert seemed to be getting closer to becoming real. We stood waiting to hear from the front office to see if they were going to cancel the last go around.

I looked up at the dark sky. The sun, so strong just a few minutes earlier, was gone. It wasn't raining, but there was no other way this could end.

Blue jays squawked high up in the pines. I watched the water glide by. I visualized how it had looked for most of the morning. Warm with the sun threading through the thick trees along the shore, hitting the water, making it look like there were little diamonds riding the waves. I wanted to remember it like this through the upcoming fall and winter.

Ty came up from behind and wrapped his strong arms around me.

He was his old self and wasn't upset at me anymore about Paloma. I promised him that in the future I would just tell him about those things right away. And then it would be on him.

"So what do you think?" he said. "Wanna come?

Ty was going backpacking up in the mountains, hiking in about eight or nine miles and spending the night. I wanted to go but was still thinking about it. Being in a tent all night with Ty made me nervous. More than nervous.

My heart raced and I was quiet.

He held me tightly and whispered in my ear.

"Come with me, Abby. It'll be a great night, I promise. I'll take care of you up there."

His gentle words sent an electric current up and down my arms and back.

"Plus, I'll carry all the heavy stuff."

"Well, that was a given," I said.

"Do I scare you that much?" he said after a moment of silence.

"Yes." I laughed nervously. "But I was just thinking about work. I'd have to get the time off. You know, Mike already scheduled me. I don't know. I guess I could ask him."

"Okay," he said. "Let me know. I want you to be there."

Amber announced that we were approved for the final run. I finished putting the life vests in piles according to size while Ty got the rafts ready. The wind picked up and I felt a few drops. You had to expect to get a little wet out here.

Chapter 15

It was a good beginning to the new season.

We won our first game in the coolness of a clear September evening. I didn't score but had a nice assist on the game's lone goal.

I felt like my new running regimen was paying off already.

"That's how it's done," Ty said, clapping from the sidelines. "Great game!"

"Yeah," I said. "That was all right."

"You guys meeting us, right?" Tim said, walking up. "We're stopping over at McMenamins for a victory beer."

I looked over at Ty and he nodded.

"Sure," I said.

"I'll get us a table in the back by the fire pit. See you guys in about half an hour."

I stretched for a few minutes.

"I like watching you play," Ty said. "You're really good out there."

I smiled.

We drove over and found the team. They were in the back, by the pit like Tim said, already with pints in front of them, talking in a large circle. We joined them.

"Ty, you should play with us," Sam said. "Victor sprained his ankle last week. We have an opening."

Ty laughed.

"No way. I would sprain more than that if I actually had to play in a game."

We didn't have instant replay, but we did have Tim. He relived his goal for us, from several different angles, in super slow motion.

"I knew their goalie was super aggressive, so I figured I'd use that against him. I just waited for him to commit himself."

"You totally outwitted that guy," Bree said. "It was awesome."

"It's just the beginning," he said. "But it's nice to get off to a good start. I tell you what. There's nothing like winning. I think we can all appreciate how good it feels after last season."

"Well, we didn't have Jack last season," Bree said. "That would have made a difference."

I hadn't thought about Jack that much lately. And because no one on the team had mentioned him in a long time, I sometimes forgot that they still didn't know what had really happened, that he had kidnapped me and taken me to a remote island where Nathaniel Mortimer was waiting. They still thought of him as a friend and a good guy.

"For sure he would have gotten us into the playoffs," she said.

I looked over at her, but didn't say anything.

"Doubt it," Ty said to my surprise.

"What?" she said. "What are you talking about? Did you even know Jack?"

"I think I know him a lot better than you," he said.

"You know nothing," Bree said. "And you have no right to say that about our friend."

I looked away at the fire and then at the people at the next table, hoping Ty was done, but he wasn't.

"I do know him. Jack is a shapeshifter."

"What are you talking about now?" she said loudly.

"He's like a character from Native American mythology. A character that changes form. He pretends to be one thing, then another, then another. No one knows who he really is. That's your Jack."

No one said anything, their eyes shifting from Ty to Bree and then over to me.

I stared at the flames that were shooting up toward the sky, the smell of wood burning in my nostrils. I wasn't sure how to feel. While I hated talking about Jack, I hated it even more that they all thought that he was a great guy. Maybe it was time for them to know the truth.

"You're really out of line, Ty," Bree said. "He was a big part of this team and he was our friend."

"He wasn't Abby's friend," he said.

I swallowed some beer, wishing it was something stronger, and watched Bree. It seemed like she was ready to turn this into an all-out brawl, but instead sank back and just glared at Ty.

"Ty's right," I finally said. "About everything. Jack was no friend to me."

Ty smiled, his face glowing in the firelight. I looked back over at Tim. He was quiet and stared at me for a minute, like he was trying to figure things out.

"Yeah, right," Bree whispered under her breath as she got up and left.

"So did something happen between you and Jack?" Tim asked, breaking through the silence that followed.

I nodded.

"Yeah," I said. "He's bad news. Real bad. I can't get into the details right now. For the time being, you'll just have to take my word for it. Or not."

Tim adjusted his black-rimmed glasses.

"All right, I guess," he said, scratching behind his ear. "I suppose it's possible, people having different sides to them. Like in that old Brando film, *One-Eyed Jacks*."

That's exactly what Jack was. A one-eyed jack. And like Rio in the movie, I had seen the other side of his face.

"Ready?" I asked Ty after a while, a warm sensation rippling through me as I glanced at him. He was quiet, deep in thought, and staring up at the sky.

"Yep," he said.

We said goodbye to the others and walked to his truck.

"Are you tired?" he asked.

"No, not really," I said. "Why?"

"I want to show you something."

Chapter 16

We drove out to the highway and unrolled the windows as we headed out of town, gliding down US 20 and cutting deep into the desert.

I sent a text to Kate to let her know I'd be late.

"Thanks," I said to Ty after I put my phone away. "What you said about Jack. It meant a lot that you said those things to the team."

"I'm glad you're not mad. I was worried you might be. But I couldn't do it, Abby. I couldn't sit there and listen to stories about good 'ol Jack. No way."

I reached over and took his hand and kissed it.

We kept driving. Finally, he slowed down and turned off the road and into a dusty lot.

"We're here," he said.

We were the only ones around. I knew we were somewhere in the Badlands. We got out of the truck into the pitch black night.

"I come here sometimes," he said. "You know. Late at night. When it's clear like this."

My heart skipped a few beats and my breathing was shallow.

"Really?" I asked, as he moved closer.

"I come to look at the stars. I do a lot of thinking. About you. About us. It's a good place for it."

He brought down the bed of the truck and hopped up and then offered me his hand. I took it, hoping he wouldn't notice how much I was shaking.

"Cold?" he asked.

It wasn't from the cold.

"No," I said, staring up into his face, finding his eyes. They were large, full of passion. "Not really."

But he grabbed the blanket anyway and wrapped it around me. He kissed me, perfect and tender.

"I wanted you to see this," he said, looking up. "But it's only a preview of what it'll be like up in the mountains. I hope you can make it."

It was dead quiet, our heavy breathing the only sound in the desert night. He leaned over and we kissed again and then he looked up.

I followed his eyes and finally understood why we were out here. It was the sky.

"It's amazing," I said.

It really was. The sky was out in front of us, horizon to horizon. Black and full of more stars than you could count in a year.

"Wow," I said. "Man, oh, man."

"Best planetarium around. That you can drive to any-way," he said. "I've been wanting to bring you out here all summer."

I laughed for no reason and knew that he could tell how nervous I was. I wanted to be with him, could feel the pin-pricks on my flesh, could feel his fast white energy on my skin, pulling me closer, drawing me in.

"I love you, Abby," he whispered in my ear. The words hung between us as he waited for me to say something. I hugged him again, unable to speak.

I tried, but the words didn't come out. I felt it, I knew it. But I couldn't tell him. I couldn't say them. It was such an incredible night, full of love, full of desire. But those words. I couldn't say them.

We looked back up at the sky.

I smiled shyly and tried to breathe.

"My dad used to take us out camping a lot when we were kids back home," he said. "He loves astronomy. He taught us all about the stars and planets and black holes. He made each of us learn about one of the constellations and then we had to teach the others for the next time we were out."

"That's so cool," I said.

"So your dad wasn't around at all when you were growing up?"

I had told Ty about our dad, about how he had left when I was a baby.

"Nope," I said. "Never knew him at all. He just left."

"Left?" Ty repeated. "What an ass."

"Kate never talks about him. She packed away all his pictures. All she's really told me was that he broke Mom's heart and did some bad things. That's it."

"Wow," Ty said. "That must be hard."

I nodded and let my head fall onto his shoulder.

"You asked me once about my religion," he said. "This is it. The stars and planets, the trees. The river. This is where I'm happiest, where I can breathe. Where everything makes sense to me. Where I get my answers."

I understood what Ty was saying, because most of the time, I felt the same way. Being out in nature, out on the river all day, reached me in ways nothing else could. It helped balance things, make them right. I lost my darkness when I was in nature.

"I know what you mean," I said. "I feel like that too, sometimes anyway."

"I know. I can tell that you get this. I find that pretty amazing especially since you almost drowned in a lake."

"Well, technically I did drown."

He kissed me again and I melted into him. We kissed for a long time under those stars, that sky, his hand caressing my hair and then dropping down to my waist and pulling me into him.

The wind rushed through the junipers and an owl hooted in the distance.

We sat for a moment longer quietly soaking in the night. I looked back up at the stars, trying to shake off the emotions that were pooling inside.

"It's late," he said.

He helped me down from the truck and closed the back of the bed. He put his lips on my mouth again, the cool empty land vast around us.

"I had a great time, Ty," I said when he dropped me off back home. "I loved looking at the stars with you. It was..." I paused, searching for the right word. "Magical."

He nodded, but I could tell he was troubled about something, that something was on his mind. I closed the door over and the truck's light went out and we sat quiet for a moment.

"I know when you give your heart to someone it's not a small thing," he said. "It's the biggest thing. The hardest thing, to love someone like that, to give them everything you have. Everything that matters."

I nodded.

"And I know that you are sensitive and see worlds around you that I can't see. I know that you're unsure of us in that way."

"I'm not unsure of you."

"And I know that you still love Jesse, and that you feel like you'll betray him if you're with me."

"It's not exactly like—"

"Listen, Abby," he said. "I'm here. I'm alive. And I'm crazy mad in love with you. I think about you on the river,

I think about you before I fall asleep. When I wake up. When I'm out looking at the stars. When I shouldn't be thinking about you, I'm thinking about you. And all I want is to be with you. For us to be together. That's all I can think about. It burns inside sometimes."

I didn't know what to say.

"But I can't settle," he said. "I can't have just a part of you. I want, I need, all of you. I'll wait for you forever if I really have a chance. If you're really able to move on. But if you gave your heart to him and you can't take it back, you need to let me know so I can find a way to release this, this... hold you have on me."

I inhaled as I sat there, lost in his words. There was so much to say, so much I needed to tell him. That I did love him, that I never wanted him to release me. All these thoughts flew through my head, spinning and spinning and not able to come out. Stuck, stuck, stuck, right there in my throat, even with his desperate eyes locked onto mine, waiting for me to say it. To say something.

But I couldn't.

I stayed quiet. Again.

"Good night," I said finally, my heart pounding in my ears, as I leaned over and kissed him on the cheek.

"Good night, Abby," I heard him whisper sadly.

It wasn't the way the night was supposed to end.

Chapter 17

The morning dragged, not because I was tired from being out late with Ty, but because of the growing guilt over not being able to tell him how I really felt about him.

And an eight-hour shift at Back Street wasn't helping any.

I finished unpacking the boxes in the back before taking my lunch, trying to focus on all the money I was making for my trip to Barcelona.

I checked my phone and saw that I had missed a call from Paloma. She left a message apologizing.

I thought about Ty and his sad, lonely eyes as he drove away last night. I hoped he wasn't still upset.

"Hey, you guys going to the Brandi Carlile concert next week?" David asked as I walked over to the door.

"No," I said. "The guides are having our end-of-the-season party over at Amber's house that night."

"Are you talking about Amber Svenson who lives over on Delaware Avenue?"

"Yeah, that's the one. Do you know her?"

"Oh, yeah. She's a party animal. I see her out all the time."

I laughed, wondering if he was just joking. She didn't seem like that at all. She was always quiet and reserved out on the river.

"No way," I said.

"Total way. Late night, at the clubs, she's a beast. But the parties at her house suck big wang. I've been. Trust me, it'll wrap up by 10. Just meet us afterwards. We're starting at Velvet about that time."

"Yeah, I guess we could do that," I said. "Sounds fun."

"Damn right I'm fun."

Kate pulled up and waited with the car running.

"Say hi to Sista Craig," he said, a little hurt. "I see she's avoiding me."

"I will. See you after lunch."

I opened the car door, a wave of cold air greeting me.

"Hey," Kate said.

"You look the part," I said, staring at her jewelry and lipstick. "Press conference or interview?"

"Interview," she said. I looked down at her shoes.

"Wow, must be a big story for the Choos to come out," I said.

"It is Choo worthy."

She smiled and shifted gears and we zoomed down Columbia.

"Did you have a good time last night?"

"Yeah, it was pretty good," I said quickly. "But right now I'm more excited to see what's for lunch."

A picnic in the park was her idea and I smiled as we sat down and she started bringing out the items from a paper bag.

"Not your school lunch, that's for sure," I said. There were falafels, hummus, pitas, sliced tomatoes and cucumbers, and plain yogurt.

We sat eating, not saying much, watching the kids play and people walking around. It was a nice day, warm and clear. The dried grass dancing in the breeze, the sunflowers in full bloom by the side of the river.

When we finished, I leaned my arms on the table. Maybe she could help.

"It was a good night," I sighed. "But there's this weird thing it ended with."

"What happened?" she asked, putting the little cartons back in the sack.

"Well, it's this stupid thing I'm having trouble telling him. Ty tells me that he loves me, and I can't say anything. I freeze. And now I've hurt his feelings. It's a mess. And I think it has to do with…"

I stopped, hoping she'd say something. But she waited for me to finish.

"I can't seem to tell him how I feel. And I'm not sure why. I think maybe it has to do with…"

I paused again, watching a lone kayaker paddling downriver.

"Jesse?" Kate said.

I looked at her.

"Yeah. Jesse."

I put on my sunglasses, hiding my glassy eyes.

"Jesse was your first love. It's always like that. That's how it works, whether they're alive or dead. When you love someone like you did Jesse that love will always be there. But it's okay to love someone else, too. You don't have to stop loving Jesse to be with Ty, Abby."

I sighed.

"It feels like it," I said. "That if I'm going to be with Ty, I'm ending it with Jesse."

Kate rubbed my shoulder.

"Abby, it ended with Jesse the day he died in the car crash. He's not here anymore."

I wiped my eyes.

"And you're going to have to either accept it or not, but if you don't, you'll probably be letting go of Ty. Nobody wants to compete with a ghost. It's impossible. Jesse would have wanted you to live your life."

I realized Kate was only trying to help. She was painting it black and white. But I could see a third color in all this.

Gray.

And gray can be a very complicated color.

Chapter 18

I drove over to the Bend Historical Society, which was across the street from the library. I had seen the old brick building hundreds of times without giving it a second thought. It was Kate's idea to check into the history of Club 6 and what was there before. She had already looked into the bar's recent past but hadn't uncovered anything conclusive.

I turned into the parking lot and got out. Paloma was waiting for me in front. She had her hands stuffed in her jean pockets and was looking down at a crack in the sidewalk.

"Sorry I'm a little late," I said.

She looked up and smiled.

"Oh, that's okay. Thanks for doing this. I'm sorry again for freaking out the other night. But he had never been that close before. He was in the cage with me. Those eyes. The things behind them. I had to get out."

She looked tired. But she seemed in control of her emotions. Like the way she had been when I'd met her over at the track. More or less normal.

"Don't worry about it," I said. "I'm not really an expert at seeing spirits or anything. Maybe there was something I missed at the bar."

I put it out there, mostly to make her feel better. It was true. I knew I still had a lot to learn, but I had confidence in what I saw or didn't see. My abilities weren't scientific or anything. But at the same time, I'd been seeing spirits for several years now. I hoped it wasn't the case, but Paloma's ghost may only have been in her head.

We walked up to the counter and an old woman with gray hair and dark-rimmed glasses greeted us. She looked at us strangely for a moment. Maybe it was because of our ages. I doubted anyone under fifty ever came into the place.

"May I help you?"

"Yes, I called earlier about the history surrounding the Club 6 building," I said.

She gave me the slightest of nods. Then she bent over and reached under the counter. A moment later she handed me a file stuffed with papers and old clippings.

"You can read this in that room," she said, pointing to a door behind us. "But you can't take anything from this file out of this building. If you need a copy of something, just let me know. They're 25 cents per page."

I thanked her and grabbed the folder and we went over to the room. Dark carpeting covered the floor. There was a strong musty smell inside, like we had stepped into the oldest room in Oregon.

Paloma sat down next to me.

"I've never been to one of these places," she said, setting her bag on the table.

"Me neither."

She rubbed her arms.

"Kind of gives me the heevy jeevies," she said.

"The what?"

C'mon, girl. You know what I'm saying. *Piel de gallina*. Goose bumps. The creeps. The willies. The heevy jeevies."

"Oh, the heevy jeevies," I said. "Why didn't you say so?"

"I did."

We both smiled. It was the first real smile I'd seen from her. I wondered if this was how she normally was before she began being haunting.

I opened the file and we shuffled through the papers. They were arranged chronologically. There were old newspaper stories from *The Bugler* about the building that went as far back as 1910.

I plowed through some of the polite phrasing of the time and got the gist hidden between the lines. We read a few of the articles, trading them when we had finished, and after a few minutes reached the same conclusion.

"So back then it was called the Silver Dollar and, what, it was a place for ladies of the night or something?" Paloma said.

"Yeah," I said. "It sounds like it was a brothel. They used the Club 6 area as a bar and the upstairs rooms were... you know. The brothel part."

"Club 6 feels shady as shit sometimes. But I had no idea it used to be a whorehouse."

For a moment I tried to imagine what things must have been like in Bend 100 years ago.

"So, Abby, what do you do when you're not making coffee or ghostbusting?" she said, looking up at me.

"Ghostbusting?"

"You know, *Ghostbusters* was one of my favorite movies growing up. Me and my sister must have watched it a hundred times. Bill Murray's so cool. Still."

"When he's on there's no one better," I said. "Anyway, when I'm not playing Dr. Peter Venkman or river guiding on the Deschutes I'm usually playing soccer."

"*Orale.*"

"How do you do it?" I asked her. It had been on my mind since visiting the club. "I mean how do you get up in that cage and dance like that?"

"After a while you don't think about it. The people looking at you and all that. I didn't look around when I first started, but after a while I noticed that most of them don't even look at me and if they do it's usually for just a few seconds. Now I just get lost in the music and tune the rest of it out. I imagine it probably isn't that different from when you play soccer. I mean, when you're on and feeling it, I bet you don't notice much else."

"I guess," I said.

We went back to the file. There was another article that mentioned the owner of the Silver Dollar, a man named Clyde Tidwell. He had been shot in the head and killed during a heated poker game.

I handed the story to Paloma.

"This is some real Wild West stuff right here," she said.

A minute later she handed me one of the other clippings. Her hand was trembling.

It was a story about the murder of one of the prostitutes. She had been strangled. The story said that the killing followed the same pattern of two earlier murders. The police had no suspects.

We kept reading, but didn't find any other mention of the murder of the three women. I assumed the killer was never caught.

Near the bottom of the file I found a photo of one of the victims. Her name was Inez Morales. I blinked hard in disbelief. She looked a lot like Paloma.

It wasn't just because they were both Hispanic. The woman had short hair, which I thought was unusual for back then. She appeared to be around Paloma's age. And there was something about the eyes.

I wasn't sure if the stale air of the place had gotten to me, but the more I looked at the picture the more I felt like they were dead ringers.

Paloma didn't seem to notice the resemblance, so I let it go. I didn't need to add that worry to her plate on top of everything else she was going through.

We finished reading and learned that the building housed a restaurant after Tidwell's death. Following that it became a country western bar. From the 1970s up through Club 6, several different bars had come and gone in the spot, none staying for very long.

From the accounts it seemed like there was always violence associated with the place. Fights and stabbings and assaults plagued whatever establishment set up shop there.

"It seems cursed," Paloma said.

At the very bottom of the pile, there was an old photo of the Silver Dollar from the early 1900's. Several men were standing out in front, dressed in top hats and clothing from that era. The photo was grainy, and their faces were hard to make out. All I could really tell was that no one was smiling. They just all stared at the camera, serious, hollow expressions on their faces.

I always thought there was something unnerving about old photos. How no one ever smiled in them.

I pushed it over to Paloma.

"Do you recognize any of them?" I said.

She studied the picture for a long time, looking into the face of each of the men. Finally, she let out a long sigh.

"I can't tell," she said. "I want to… I want to recognize one of them so bad, Abby. But I just can't tell. The photo's too old."

I nodded.

"So what does this mean?" she asked.

"I don't know," I said, trying to hide my disappointment at not having found something more concrete. "I think it's a good start."

"Does that mean you believe me? Even though you can't see him, you believe me that I see a ghost?"

I hesitated for a moment with my answer. I wanted it to sound right.

"I think it's possible. I didn't see him, but like I said, I'm not a professional. There's still a lot I don't know about that world. Maybe he's able to show himself just to you for some reason. I don't know. I don't know how it all works over there."

Paloma looked down and nodded.

"That means a lot, Abby," she said. Her voice shook a little, like she was trying to swallow back tears. "Everyone else just thinks I'm crazy."

"I know how that feels," I said.

I organized the clippings and put them back in the folder. We left the room, and I placed the file back on the counter where the old lady came out to retrieve it.

"Did you find what you were looking for?" she asked.

"Some of it," I said. "Thank you for your help."

She nodded. We walked out the door.

It felt good to get outside into the bright sunlight, away from that stagnant air.

"Well, thanks again, Abby," Paloma said as we walked to the parking lot.

"I'm going to think about what we learned today and maybe run it by a friend of mine who knows more than I do," I said. "I'll call you. Hang in there."

"You mean in my cage?" She smiled.

She got into her car and brought down her window.

"It's weird. I know we didn't find much, but I feel a little bit better about it all," she said. "Maybe everything's going to be okay."

She started up the engine and backed out. She turned up the stereo and Christina Aguilera started screaming. I waved at her as she pulled out of the lot.

"I hope so," I said when she was down the street. "I hope you're right."

At first I wanted to help Paloma because it was the right thing to do. But it was becoming more than that. It was becoming personal. I liked her. I liked her a lot.

Chapter 19

The customers were well behaved and all the runs were smooth.

I had time to think about Paloma and what we had discovered at the historical society. It wasn't much really. Nothing that left me feeling like we were any closer to finding out who her ghost was or what he wanted. I supposed that, if he was real, he might not even be connected to Club 6. For all I knew, he could have attached himself to her somewhere else.

I knew it was too early to start feeling hopeless. But on the other hand, the more I thought about it, the harder it became to find any evidence that I was making progress. The whole thing was beginning to take on a dead in the water feeling.

We ran through Big Eddy and the kids in my group screamed and laughed all the way through. I had two families in the raft, three little kids. I kept the youngest one close to me.

"We had a great time," the dad said afterwards, walking back over to me while his family climbed up into the bus. He handed me a tip and I thanked him.

"Have you done this a long time?" he asked.

"This is my second year," I said.

"Lucky," he said. "I'm back at work on the 16th floor on Monday. Thanks again."

I stood there as the bus pulled out, a cloud of dust trailing behind it as it made its way toward the highway. A hawk circled overhead. I inhaled the sweet air and walked to the van heading back up to meet the new group.

I *was* lucky.

I would miss the river.

I would miss it a lot.

Chapter 20

Choice was the wrong word. It implied closing doors, eliminating certain things, leaving someone out. So I didn't make a choice. Instead, I made a decision.

After work I drove over to Ten Barrel to tell Ty. I sat at a table outside.

"I'll go get him," Cliff said when he saw me.

Large thunder clouds blew by quickly up above, a strong wind pushing them. I watched Ty as he made his way toward me from across the restaurant. He looked happy. And when he smiled, it sent those familiar chills down my back.

"Hey," he said. "This is a surprise. What's up?"

"I wanted to talk to you. Do you have a minute?"

"Sure. Everything okay?"

"Oh, yeah. Everything's fine. Great, really."

He stood, waiting.

"Do you want something?"

"Sure," I said, leaning back and trying to relax a little. "I'll take a Coke."

I was stalling already. He was back in a minute and set the glass down on the table while I fiddled with a napkin. He sat down.

"How are you doing?" I asked.

"Excellent," he said.

I took a drink.

He lowered his voice.

"You sure everything is okay?"

"Oh, yeah," I said, trying to sound relaxed. "Looks like something is blowing in."

"Maybe. Seems like it's been like this all summer. A little rumbling, but nothing too serious."

I exhaled.

"I'd like to go with you," I said finally. "You know, on your backpacking trip. If you're still going."

Our eyes locked for a moment and then he smiled.

"Really?" he said. "But I thought you couldn't get away?"

"No, I can. I mean, I did already. Mike said it wasn't a big deal. So, yes, I can come. I mean, I'd like to."

I was stuttering, nervous. He kissed me.

"It'll be nice to take a break and get some fresh mountain air," he said.

He took my hand and I smiled.

***

I had written to Claire, my psychic friend in London, shortly after the visit to the historical society, but I still hadn't heard back. I wasn't sure what she could really do from so far away, but I figured that any insight would help.

I told her everything, including the details of my visit to Club 6 and how even though Paloma saw the ghost in front of her, I hadn't been able to see anything. I also filled her in with some of the information we had learned about the building when we researched it.

I was watching an old movie and surfing around when Claire's email came in. I opened it right away.

Hi, Abby.

It certainly sounds like your friend is in a bloody awful situation, doesn't it?

It appears that she has attracted this entity somehow, and I would doubt that he will simply let her go so easily. Perhaps there's a priest or holy man in your area that could bless her? I think that would help. And if she could find another job elsewhere with the greatest of haste, I would advise that as well.

Personally, I've been very lucky in that I've had few dealings with the dark side. I make every effort to avoid it.

I have found over the years that spirits are very much like people in that there are all types floating about. Some are charming and others are sinister. We must protect ourselves from the evil ones as best we can. I make it a habit of cloaking myself in white light in my mind before approaching any dubious spirit and would advise you to do the same.

I think the strangest part of all this, Abby, is that you have not been able to see this particular spirit. It's an important element and should not be set aside. You should consider that either you are up against a very powerful entity that is able to keep you away, or perhaps it is just the sad fact that your friend is a bit barmy.

I hope some of this helps. You will let me know how all this turns out, won't you?

Cheers.

Claire

I closed my laptop and put it aside, thinking about what she wrote while I flipped through the TV stations.

From what Claire was saying, it was a lose-lose situation.

Either Paloma had a very dangerous ghost attached to her or she was crazy.

Either way, it didn't look good.

***

"Hope you guys are all right up there," Kate said, staring up at the sky.

We had heard the first thunder clap while cleaning up after dinner. I pulled the lawn chairs over to the patio so we could watch the storm protected from the rain.

"Yeah, me too," I said. "But it's getting to be now or never. The hiking season up there is just for a few more weeks, unless you don't mind camping in the snow."

I kicked off my sandals.

"Boy, those are thrashed," Kate said, looking at them.

"Yeah. I'll have to get some more for next year."

"So you're signing on again, huh?" she asked.

"Think so."

There was a long time between here and next summer and there was a chance that I would try something else, something more like a career. Someday I'd have to think about my plans for the future.

Lightning streaked across the sky, followed by distant thunder as we watched two squirrels jumping through the garden, playing and chasing each other.

"Thunderstorms are the best," Kate said. "Reminds me of when we were kids. Remember? Mom would always sit with us out here and watch."

"Yeah," I said. "I remember. Hey, I called the restaurant and scheduled my classes. I start in a few weeks."

Kate had bought me a month's worth of Italian cooking classes for my birthday from a local chef who owned a restaurant in town. I had been too busy to start, but now I had some time and was really looking forward to it.

"Awesome," she said.

"Thanks, Kate. I can't wait."

It was nice sitting back here, with not much to do. Ty said he was packing everything up, that all I had to do was be ready.

"Backyard looks really nice this year," I said. "The pond, and all the flowers. It's very peaceful out here."

I put my feet up on the small wooden table. Another flash streaked down, this time in a jagged vertical line. The thunder followed, sharp and loud.

"So what time are you heading out tomorrow?"

"Nine."

A strong gust blew past us, knocking over a stack of empty plastic plant containers by the side of the house and scattering them across the yard. As Kate ran to collect them, a few drops fell out of the sky.

Chapter 21

The next morning it looked as though there had never even been a storm, with only a few wispy clouds stretched faintly across the sky.

"How does it feel?" Ty asked after we walked a few feet. He had given me a small pack while he had a huge one on his back.

"Oh, it's so heavy," I said. "Could you take a few more things?"

He laughed.

"Anything you want," he said. "So, really, it feels okay?"

"Come on, it's like the pack's empty. Even Kate makes me carry more than this when we go out on a day hike. Seriously, give me a few more things."

"Keep walking," he said.

The air was cool as we hiked along the dirt trail, following the stream past loud waterfalls and small meadows. The path kept climbing up, eventually meeting the first Green Lake at the base of South Sister, with Broken Top to the right, where we took a candy bar break.

"Beautiful," Ty said.

We took off our shoes, sat down by the lake, and soaked our feet in the cold water.

"I haven't been up here in a while," I said. "But it's just like I remember it."

Ty took some pictures before we got back on the trail. We made it up to Golden Lake by late afternoon, the sun slanted in the sky, the warm glow catching the grasses just right. Ty pulled out the tent and we set it up in a small grove of trees off to the side, next to a meadow. We seemed to have the place to ourselves.

"Are you hungry?" he asked.

"Starved. What's for dinner?"

"It's a surprise," he said.

"I can help."

"Nope," he said, unpacking gear. "It's my turn to show off my culinary skills. You just relax."

He brought out the stove and set up a makeshift kitchen on a flat rock while I headed down to a small stream and pumped some water. I washed my face and hands, the water cold on my cheeks.

It felt good to be here.

While Ty worked on dinner, I walked over to the lake and stared out at it. It was small, a few ripples rolling in the wind, sparkling in the last of the fading sun.

When I came back, Ty handed me a paper plate. He had made a pesto linguini, with a sprinkling of extra pine nuts and cheese on top.

"You made all this now?" I said, sopping the sauce up with a slice of bread.

"I made the pesto last night," he said.

"I didn't even know you could cook."

"Just out here," he said. "I get inspired. I found this recipe online, a site for cooking in the woods. This is pretty damn good, huh?"

"It's beyond damn," I said, smiling.

I looked out across the lake.

"So is it really true there aren't any bears out here?"

"I'm not sure if every single one is gone, but I think most are," I said.

"That's kind of weird. What about mountain lions?"

"Yeah," I said. "We have some of those. Even over at Pilot Butte sometimes."

We cleaned up and gathered sticks and branches as the sun sank behind Middle Sister and crisp, cool air fell around us. I made a ring with small rocks and we got a fire going. We sat there on a log, our breaths foggy in front of us, mixing together and vanishing in the flames and embers.

"It's going to be a perfect night for the stars," he said. "It's a new moon."

He got up and grabbed the sleeping bags, laying them side by side close to the fire.

He started talking about his childhood in Montana and riding horses, about his dad and growing up on a ranch.

"Do you ride?" he asked, picking up a stick and breaking it, throwing the pieces one by one into the fire.

I laughed.

"Just in circles at birthday parties," I said. "It's been a while."

"Maybe we'll go sometime. Maybe you'll come back to the ranch."

The first stars twinkled above as we fed the fire. When the sky was black and full of stars, our conversation slowed.

I took a breath, trying to calm my nerves.

"It's so beautiful out here," I said, looking up.

"Nothing compared to you," he said, staring at me.

He moved closer and kissed me. When we pulled away, I looked into his eyes as the flames danced in the reflection.

"I love you, Ty," I said.

The words flowed, even and naturally. I whispered in his ear in between heavy breaths.

"I love you so much," I said, wrapping my arms around him.

His eyes softened, softer than I'd ever seen.

"I've been waiting a long time to hear those words, Abby."

"I didn't think I could. I didn't think I could love anyone again. But I do. I love you with all my heart."

My feelings were strong and steady as our lips met, our bodies close, our hearts beating together. I couldn't deny them anymore, couldn't stop them either.

I inhaled, breathing him in, shaking, the words powerful and passionate, falling into the flames and turning into smoke to spread out far into the universe. I took his hand and placed it on my chest.

"My heart is yours now."

He kept it there and stared for a long time into my eyes, not saying anything.

"You belong with me, Abby." His voice was soft, but urgent. "I won't let you down. Not ever. Trust me tonight."

I trusted him with everything.

My heart, my soul, our love.

He kissed me again and pulled at my shirt. I let it fall to the ground as his hands moved over my body, soft and tender, the fire crackling loud in my ears, the night gathering in around us.

He pulled me to him and I sank inside his white energy, lost, and then taken.

Taken, wrapped in his love, under a sky bursting with burning stars.

Chapter 22

It was pitch black outside when we walked over to the lake. It was the most brilliant sky I had ever seen in my life. Ty wrapped his arms around me as he stood behind me, whispering in my ear.

"I love you, Abby," he said.

"I love you, too," I said, surprised at the ease now of the words that used to be so hard.

We stood there quiet for a while, listening to the sound of the mountains. Grass blowing in the wind, frogs croaking in the lake.

"You're shaking," he said. "Are you cold?"

I had on my thick fleece jacket, but it wasn't enough.

"A little," I said.

He took off his jacket and put it on me.

"Thanks," I said.

"It was incredible," he said in a low voice. "I hope it was—"

"It was," I said, letting my head fall back onto his chest. I touched his arms with my hands, brushing the small hairs that were standing up. "It was, Ty."

He was quiet, looking up.

"There it is. Andromeda," he said, pointing up. "That's the constellation that reminds me of us. And there's Perseus."

He took my hand and we traced the outline together.

"Why?" I asked.

"Because of the story," he said, leading me back to the fire.

"In Greek times Andromeda was a princess who lived with her mother and father in a kingdom by the sea. Her mother was very proud of her and bragged to everyone that her daughter was the most beautiful girl in the entire world."

"Uh, oh," I said. "Bragging like that is never good in Greek mythology."

"Nope, never is," he said. "Poseidon was furious when he heard about what the queen had said because he thought his sea nymphs were the most beautiful creatures in the world. So to teach her a lesson, he sent huge waves toward the kingdom to destroy it. And then he sent a sea monster."

I moved a little closer to the fire.

"Soon the king heard about Poseidon's anger and was at a loss as to what to do. He consulted the oracles and they told him that there was only one way. He would have to sacrifice his daughter to the sea monster to satisfy Poseidon.

"So the king had Andromeda chained to the rocks.

"A young man named Perseus happened to be walking by when he came upon the beautiful princess tied down. He fell in love with her at first sight and vowed to save her. And just as the monster was about to attack, he killed it. He untied Andromeda and asked for her hand in marriage."

Ty smiled, his face glowing as he stared at me.

"So you're Perseus?" I asked, looking back up at the constellation.

"Yep," he said.

I was quiet for a moment.

"And you think I need saving?" I said.

"Everybody needs a little saving now and then. That's part of love, isn't it?"

"I guess so."

I stared into the flames.

"So what happened to them, Perseus and Andromeda?"

"They lived happily ever after and loved each other forever. And because their love was so pure and special, the Gods placed them in the heavens for all time. They're up there to remind us about what's important."

"That's a good story," I said.

"It is," Ty said.

We stared up at the black sky above us, where everything seemed so real and free.

Chapter 23

In the morning a light frost had coated everything. I woke up and stepped outside of the tent and found Ty standing in the meadow.

I walked up to him and put my arm around his waist.

"Look at this place. It's stunning," I said.

The early morning sun was hitting the tip of Broken Top, the jagged peaks bright in the light.

***

"So how was your wilderness trip?" David asked, handing me paper towels across the counter so I could clean up the spill in the corner. "And don't leave anything out."

I wiped down the table and walked back to the register, taking a few orders.

"So?" he asked again when it had quieted down.

"It was a great trip," I said.

"More."

"We had a really good time," I said finally, refusing to meet his probing eyes.

"Um, hmmm. Thought so," he said. "You seem stupid happy, Abby Craig, and I can tell that you're in love."

I still didn't look at him, but he hovered near me anyway, staring. I could feel my lips break out in a smile no matter how much I tried to stop it and he laughed.

"It's beautiful up there," I said. "You know, you might want to get outdoors once in a while, go on a walk or something. We do live in this incredible place."

"Forget it," he said. "You're preaching to the lazy."

I laughed and took a tray of dirty cups to the back. When I came out, Lyle was working the register and David had moved behind the machines.

"So, it's not like love or anything, but I met someone too," he said, screaming over the whirl of the steamer. "A hottie visiting from Portland."

"That's great," I said.

"Yeah, at least he's not far if things heat up. Hey, we're going out tonight, if you want to meet up at Club 6 or something."

I was pretty sure Ty wouldn't be so excited about going back there.

"Maybe," I said. "I'll let you know. I have a game tonight."

"How's the new season going?" he asked.

"I have a good feeling about it."

Chapter 24

The FedEx package was on the front porch when I got home from work.

It was a box of gardenias, arriving just in time. I picked it up, fumbled for my keys, and sighed.

It was hot inside, the air stagnant. I put the parcel on the table and opened some windows, letting the breeze blow through the house. I changed and brought my laptop out to the dining room table and turned it on.

She would have been 51 tomorrow. Even with all the time that had passed, that was still young. Too young to have that first part always attached now to her birthday. "She would have been…"

Sometimes I dreamed of her and most of the time they were good dreams. She looked healthy, like how I remembered her when I was in elementary school. Her hair long, down her back, and her face full of life and energy.

And that smile. She was always smiling.

It's when I'm awake that I have to chase away those other images.

Her thin, gray body lying on hospital sheets, with tubes and wires attached everywhere. Vases of wilting flowers pushed to the corner of the room.

Kate and I sleeping in chairs near her bed.

That doctor.

"It wasn't what she would have wanted," Kate yelled, her voice strong and fragile at the same time. "Just take the damn tubes out!"

I stood there, not saying anything, watching like it was a movie. Too numb and destroyed to beg him. The doctor shook his head, glancing at the chart he was holding. He knew there was no hope.

Later that day, he did it. We sat stroking her hands, telling her how much we loved her as the quiet of the heart monitor grew. She took her final breath while we foolishly clung to the hope that she would open her eyes.

I shivered at the memory.

I was making her a playlist for her birthday. It was just Kate and me and we did it every year. We went to the graveyard and left her the gardenias. I made a lemon cake and we brought out the old photo albums and listened to some of her favorite songs.

She loved Bruce Springsteen, the old songs. *Spirit in the Night, Growing Up, Born to Run, Thunder Road, Point Blank*. As I created the playlist, I remembered that one rainy night.

"Come on, girls," she said, turning the stereo up loud. "Katie, Abby! Dance with me! It's Bruce. Come on!"

Kate rolled her eyes and took the phone into the kitchen. But I loved dancing with Mom. I met her in the middle of the living room and we moved fast to *Rosalita*, sweating and laughing and almost crashing into the TV a couple of times.

When it ended, a slow song came on. She ran over to the stereo and I thought she was going to skip it, but instead she turned it up even louder.

She grabbed me and we started dancing slow.

Bruce's sad voice echoed throughout the house, full of longing as he sang about loss and old love letters that made one of the characters in the song feel a hundred years old.

She wrapped her arms around me tighter and I put my head on her chest, her voice vibrating through my body as she sang along.

The song ended with a confession. The singer was afraid that in "this darkness I will disappear."

We rocked back and forth, back and forth to the slow, haunting beat, like no darkness would ever touch us.

Chapter 25

"You won't believe what they're expecting me to wear," David said as we roamed up and down the aisles at Ross. He was looking for an outfit for his upcoming play, the one where he only had a few lines.

"They handed me something that Lyle would wear. And it looks like it's just as old as he is, too."

I gave him a look.

"Seriously, it's dusty and just hangs there on me. I don't know who they think I am. If I'm going out on stage, even in some lame minor role, I'm going to look bad ass."

I laughed as I held up a shirt for him to consider.

"Nah," he said, shaking his head. "Too western. Remember, it's a serious story set in Kansas City in the 1940s. I'm looking for something, I don't know. I'll know it when I see. And I'm not seeing it."

I put it back on the rack.

"So, remember too that I can't really spend as much as I was hoping. I went all drunk millionaire last night."

I looked at him.

"You know. When you get so drunk that you keep buying rounds at the bar? It's cut into my costume budget."

It was fun being with him away from work.

"So that's really cool that your mom's coming out for the play. That's a long trip."

David's family all lived in Maine. I was never too sure why he had moved to Oregon. The few times he began to tell me, the story meandered around so much that I never got a real explanation.

"Yeah," he said, sounding a little sad.

"Don't you get along with her?".

"Oh, it's not that," he said. "Let's go look at shoes."

He pointed out a bunch of shoes, all with three inch heels on them.

"Abby Craig, it's time to say goodbye to those river sandals."

"I thought we were shopping for you," I said. "And anyway, what's going on with your mom? I can see it in your energy."

He stopped and looked at me, worried.

"Oh, my gosh, really?" he said. "Well. Okay. This is how it is. I was so sure that I would get the lead role. You know, like I should have. So that's what she's expecting to see. That's why she's coming out."

I nodded.

We went back to look at more shirts.

"Isn't this color incredible, Abby Craig?" he kept saying, forgetting about my color blindness for at least the hundredth time.

We were becoming really good friends, and despite his loose mouth, I felt like I could trust him. It was nice to have someone to talk to about my abilities. It made me feel good that I had someone else other than Kate who I could be honest with about this kind of stuff, someone who didn't judge me.

"I just wish she'd be able to see me in a real production," David said, sighing and holding up a blazer. "I invited her to come out thinking I'd get the main role, not the role of Cab Driver Number One."

"Yeah, that's too bad," I said. "But I'm sure she'll love just seeing you up on stage. Plus, there's always a chance that you could still be the lead. You're the understudy, right?"

David turned to me, that signature eyebrow of his flying high.

"And don't you think I haven't thought of that," he said, lowering his voice. "You never know. Marlon might just have a…"

He looked around making sure nobody else was within earshot, then cleared his throat.

"An accident the night of the show."

He winked and after a moment of silence we both started laughing.

"It would serve him right," he said. "Any actor who calls himself *Marlon* these days has it coming to him. Don't you think? I mean, how pretentious is that?"

"So, David, I've been meaning to ask you about Club 6," I said, as he made a face while holding up a hideous checkered number.

"I'm your man," he said. "Shoot."

"I was wondering if you've ever seen anything, you know, anything odd there."

"Practically every time I've been there," he said. "That place can be a real freak scene. But it's my kind of freak scene."

He smiled.

"No. I mean, like have you ever seen something you couldn't explain? Like what Paloma's talking about? A ghost of some sort?"

David thought on it for a minute and then shrugged.

"If I did see a ghost, I didn't know I was seeing it. Anyway, by the time I wind up at that place, I'm usually a few sheets to the wind, if you know what I mean."

"Paloma says the ghost is a man in his 40s with dark hair and blue eyes. She says he likes to hover around her. Have you seen anyone like that in the club?"

I knew I was just grasping at shadows in the dark, but I figured there was no harm in asking.

"I've never seen anyone under 25 in that place," he said. "Besides, I thought you were the one who was supposed to see ghosts."

"Not this one," I mumbled. "I really want to help her, but I can't do much if I can't even see the ghost she's talking about."

"Well, don't beat yourself up over it," he said. "We can't always shine like we want to. Sometimes, we just have to settle on being cab drivers."

I laughed.

We walked over to the Halloween section.

"Maybe I can find a costume here," he said.

"Isn't it a little early for this?"

"Where's your inner child, Abby Craig? It's never too early for Halloween."

He suddenly picked up a skull with a candle on top.

"Alas, poor Yorick!" he began in a deep, booming voice. *"I knew him, Horatio: a fellow of infinite jest, of most excellent fancy: he hath borne me on his back a thousand times; and now, how abhorred in my imagination it is! My gorge rims at it."*

A few people turned and began staring. David continued.

"Here hung those lips that I have kissed I know not how oft. Where be your gibes now? your gambols? your songs? your flashes of merriment, that were wont to set the table on a roar? Not one now, to mock your own grinning? quite chap-fallen? Now get you to my lady's chamber, and tell her, let her paint an inch thick, to this favour she must come; make her laugh at that."

When he had finished, some of the people listening started clapping.

David set the skull down and took a bow.

Sometimes I forgot how good he was. He was always acting funny, but when he turned it on he had real presence. It made me wonder if the director knew anything about acting.

"You've got a real gift, David Norton," I said. "Maybe you could put on a one-man show for your mom."

"That's so nice of you to say, Abby Craig."

"No, I mean it."

"I'll give it some serious mulling over," he said excitedly. "It might be fun."

We walked back over to the shoes.

"Look!" he said, holding up a pair of plastic snakeskin cowboy boots. "Giddy up, anyone?"

I didn't have to see colors to know that they were the ugliest cowboy boots this side of Texas.

"What's Mama Norton gonna think when she sees you wearing those?" I said.

"That she did a good job raising me," he said, laughing. "Because her son is one fierce *mutha*."

Chapter 26

I was about a mile into my run when I saw him walking out from the trees at the edge of the park. I was glad to see him, but a little nervous. I didn't know what to say, or if he knew.

I took a deep breath, threw down my water bottle, and headed over to meet him.

There was something about the way he was walking toward me that reminded me of when we were kids, back in fourth grade. I flashed back on our science project and how we were talking about it as we walked to his house.

We had chosen volcanoes as our topic and we had to give a presentation to the class. I had my backpack filled with color markers and books and I was holding one of those giant white poster boards. Jesse pushed his bike alongside me, and we talked about Mt. Vesuvius.

"What's that for?" Jesse said, looking at the blank board in my hands.

He was shorter than I was back then and I used to like looking down at him.

"Duh," I said. "It's for our volcano project. I think you should draw it, being that you're the artist and will get us a good grade."

His green eyes sparkled in the sun.

"No way," he said, tugging on his cap. "We're not drawing it. We're blowing it up! We should build a volcano and I'll rig it so lava flows out the top as we give our speech. It'll be so cool."

"You know how to do that?"

"Of course. I've been building volcanoes with my dad since I was little."

I smiled at the memory as I watched him. I was surprised to see him at all. I hadn't called and was trying to figure out how to explain about Ty, how to say it right.

"Jesse," I said, pushing down the guilt. "I'm glad you're here."

"Hey, stranger," he said.

We found an empty bench and I closed my eyes, the sun warm on my face, giving me strength. When I opened them, Jesse was staring at me.

"It's okay, Craigers," he said. "Stop freaking out. I'm okay. Anyway, believe it or not, I'm not here about your love life."

I laughed nervously.

"I love you too, Jesse," I said.

"I know you do," he said. "We'll always have that. Nothing takes love away. But I'm glad you have him too."

A tear slid down my cheek.

"What's up then?" I asked, my voice cracking.

He paused, fumbling for the right words as my heart hammered in my chest.

"What is it, Jesse? Tell me."

"Something is happening around you again," he said. "I don't really know what it is, just that the energy around you is different. Darker. Something is coming up, seeping in from the sides. It's like when you were in the lake and the black water surrounded you."

I sat back and tried to calm down, thinking what it might be.

"You don't know what it's about? No idea at all?"

"No. Just that sometimes it blocks my view of you. It's been getting worse lately."

I took a breath. Then another.

"The last time you told me something like this I was kidnapped," I said, trying to push away those terrible memories that haunted me long after the fact. "Is that what's going to happen? Is this about Jack Martin? Is he back here in Bend?"

"I don't know. I'm sorry, I wish I could see more. I was just glad to have found you now. It's important that you know. You need to be prepared."

I nodded, my eyes darting back and forth at the people walking by.

I sighed and he put his arm around me and I fell back into him, scared.

"I'm tired of it," I said. "I'm tired of being in that lake. It feels like no matter how much I try to climb out of it, it sucks me back in, one way or another."

"I know," he said. "But you're not alone. I have your back. I won't let anything happen to you like that again. Not ever. I won't."

I nodded, staring at the people around us, searching.

Looking for Jack Martin.

Chapter 27

Ty and I met out in front of Amber's house for the party. I brought a red pepper dip and a few baguettes. The other guides were already there when we walked in, along with the front office staff and a few other people from the company that I didn't know that well.

Small paper lanterns and lights were strung across the front yard. The Ramones played in the background.

It was fun. We told stories and drank beer. As twilight fell it brought along cool air. There were still some warm days ahead but summer, as a long block of time and as a state of mind, felt like it was over.

We took our drinks and sat down on the sofa. I looked around. It was a small, older house with arches in the doorways and molding around all the windows. It had a lot of character. "So what color are the walls?" I asked Ty.

All I could see was that they were dark.

"Well, it's like a lot of grape stomping went on in here. All sorts of purples and reds. It's cool."

I closed my eyes and tried to remember purple. My high school soccer jersey was purple.

Hey," Ty said. "Isn't that your friend from the bar out there?"

I got up and looked outside. Someone was standing in the street, looking at the house.

"What's she doing here?" I said.

It was hard to see her face, but it was Paloma, dressed in a flowing skirt that whipped around her in the breeze. She just stood there, staring.

"I'm going to see what she wants," I said. "I'll be right back."

She must have been looking for me, but I couldn't figure out how she knew where I was.

"All right, but don't be long. I'll just be here missing you."

I walked through a cloud of cigarette smoke and passed a group of people talking loudly on the front porch.

"Hey, Pal o' mine," I said. "What are you doing here?"

She didn't say anything. She just nodded slowly and then held out her arms.

"Hey, what's wrong?"

"Look," she said, her voice cracking. Black mascara streaked down her face. "Look at what he's doing to me!"

I peered down at her arms in horror. I couldn't be seeing it right. It must have been the moonlight or my mind playing tricks.

"Oh, my God," I said.

On the inside of both arms, thick veins were bulging out of her skin from her wrists up to her elbows. And they were moving, creeping up and down, pushing up, like tiny snakes inside her. Whatever it was looked alive, using her arteries as passage ways and crawling through her body.

"It started an hour ago," she said. "He's in me, Abby! Help me! Please, help me."

"Come inside," I sputtered, not able to take my eyes off the moving veins. "Paloma. We'll get you some help. Don't worry."

"Help me! He's in here with me. He's in me, Abby!"

I could feel the heat radiating off her body. I reached out and touched her forehead. She was on fire, a torrent of sweat pouring off her face. She started coughing, slapping at her forearms.

"Paloma," I said. "Come inside. It'll be all right."

But looking at her arms I had a hard time imagining exactly how it would be all right.

"No!" she screamed, her voice echoing up and down the street. She started backing away, her crazed eyes darting back and forth.

I followed her. I could hear footsteps behind me. Ty caught up to me.

"You okay?" he said.

"Paloma's sick," I said. "She needs help!"

She screamed once more and then took off, sprinting down the dark street.

Down toward the river.

Chapter 28

We ran after her, following her down streets and alleyways. But we couldn't keep up. She was too fast and we eventually lost sight of her.

"Where'd she go? Do you see anything?"

"No," Ty said. "Let's go check the river."

The river bank was made up mostly of brush on our side and was hard to walk through. There was a park across the way. I stared at the dark black water sliding by, listening for any clues.

"Paloma!" I shouted.

"Ty, you should have seen her arms. She's really sick. We need to find her."

"It's too hard to walk over here," he said. "I'm going to cross the bridge and see if I can see anything from over there. You have your phone?"

"Yeah," I said.

He squeezed my arm before taking off toward the footbridge.

I kept looking and calling her name, slowly making my way downriver through the thick brush. I heard voices coming from the park. It didn't take Ty long to get over. I waved at him.

My phone buzzed a moment later.

"I see her, Abby," he said. "She's just around the bend, a little bit farther down from where you are. Keep going. She's standing in the water."

"What's she doing?" I said, picking up my speed.

"She's just standing there. She's just standing in the water, looking up at the sky. It's like she's praying or something."

I suddenly realized we weren't too far from the spillway.

The spillway was the sight of numerous accidents. There were plenty of warning signs posted in the water, but every year a few people, usually in inner tubes or small rafts, got sucked into the waterfall. Once in a while, someone even drowned.

"She's not far from you now," Ty said. "Can you see her?"

I spotted her a second later.

"Paloma! Get out of the water!"

She was still close to shore, her face and torso illuminated in the moonlight. But as I got closer, she suddenly dove into the river and swam out toward the center.

"Paloma!" I yelled, but it was no use. She just kept swimming downriver.

I looked over toward Ty and noticed that a small group of people were now watching.

"Paloma!"

"Don't do it!" I heard someone shout from across the way.

I glanced over and saw Ty taking off his shirt and shoes.

"No!" I shouted but he was already in the water, swimming hard toward her.

I stood there paralyzed, almost too afraid to watch.

He was closing the gap but they were heading into the section where the current picked up speed.

I finally got my legs to work and stumbled farther down the shore.

"This can't be happening," I said out loud.

A moment later he reached her, grabbing her around the waist with one arm. For a few awful seconds, the current swept them downstream, but Ty kicked furiously at the water and slowly started making progress.

If he could just reach that boulder in the middle of the river. The water flowed fast on either side of it, but if he could make it to that rock, they would be rescued. They would be all right.

I could hear a siren in the distance above the sound of my pounding heart.

If he could just make it a few more yards to that boulder, he'd be okay.

A few more strokes, Ty. Just a few more.

But he never got any closer to the boulder.

Instead, he turned and started heading for shore. Paloma didn't seem to be helping, just floating there lifelessly.

Ty started losing ground. The spillway was getting closer. They weren't going to make it.

No, Ty. No.

I screamed.

My vision blurred behind the tears. I couldn't see them anymore. First Jesse. And now Ty. *Why, God? Why!*

But the next thing I saw was Ty backstroking his way through a calmer stretch of the river. Near the far shore. Two men jumped into the water and began dragging them out onto the grass.

The siren was closer now. I ran back up to the footbridge and over to the other side. I pushed my way through the small crowd that was now surrounding them.

Ty was coughing and sputtering, trying to catch his breath. I squeezed him long and hard, his chest heaving, water dripping down my hair and face.

"Are you okay?" I said after a while.

He nodded and blinked.

"I'm gonna check on Paloma," I said.

The paramedics had arrived and were asking her questions. Her eyes were open but she didn't answer them. Then she turned and looked at me.

"Abby," she said, her eyes wide and terrified. She pulled on my hand. "What happened? Why am I all wet? Where am I?"

I put my hand on her forehead again. But she was cool now. Cold even.

"Abby, I'm so tired. I don't know what's happening."

She started sobbing quietly as the paramedics placed her on a gurney.

"You'll be okay, Paloma," I said, holding her hand. "You'll be okay."

"We're taking her to St. Charles, miss," the driver told me before they pulled away.

"Crazy shit, what that guy did, man," one teenager said. "Even for a crazy hot babe like that, I wouldn't have done that."

"He saved her," I heard a girl say. "He totally saved her."

Chapter 29

A paramedic checked Ty over and gave him a blanket. He seemed okay, but looked completely exhausted. He was drinking from a small water bottle when I went back over to him.

"How are you doing?" I asked, hugging him. "Are you really okay?"

He shrugged.

"Yeah," he said. "But I'll sleep well tonight. That's for sure."

"I was so worried, Ty," I said, my shaky voice betraying my intention to be strong for him.

"Worried?" he said. "Come on, with these guns?"

I smiled weakly.

"You saved her. She would have died if you hadn't gone in and pulled her out of the river."

"I guess. You know, she fought me at first," he said. "When I was out there swimming over to her, she was screaming at me to get away. I was just going to take her over to that rock, get her out of the current. I figured the rescue team would have ropes and it would be better to wait for them. But she was so weird. She kept saying that I wasn't in time. We were near the boulder and she looked at me with these insane eyes and then, like that, went out cold. Maybe it was the water temperature. I had to get her back."

He suddenly started shivering and I wrapped the blanket tighter around him.

"We should get you home and into a hot shower," I said.

"Let's wait a few more minutes," he said. "The cops will probably want a statement. I saw you talking to Paloma before they took her. What did she say?"

"She said she couldn't remember anything. She didn't even know what happened and was confused about where she was."

We watched as a police car pulled into the lot.

"Listen, Abby," Ty said. "Let's meet up later. Go get lost in the crowd. There's no reason you need to be here for this. You don't need any more publicity. Okay? I'll call you when I'm done."

I started to argue. I didn't want to leave him, but he insisted.

"Go," he whispered. "Before it's too late."

I kissed him hard and then walked away slowly. There were still a lot of people around, some talking to Ty and calling him a hero.

***

I saw a news van from the television station drive up. I waited in the dark for a little while before I left. A couple almost bumped into me as they stared at the flashing lights.

"Do you know what happened?" the woman said to me.

"No," I said. "No idea."

I walked over to Galveston, then up to Ten Barrel and ordered a beer. I found an empty chair outside and tried to make sense of the evening.

Paloma was burning up, that much I knew. She had a fever and seemed delirious. But what kind of illness would make her veins crawl around like that in her arms?

It was good that she was going to the hospital. Maybe the doctors would be able to come up with a logical, medical explanation.

I texted Ty, hoping he hadn't jumped into the river with his phone, and told him where I was. Then I called Kate and told her what happened.

"She would have gone over the spillway if Ty hadn't gone in after her. I'm sure of it," I said. "I think she's okay now. They took her to St. Charles."

"That's terrible," Kate said. "Do you think she tried to kill herself?"

"I dunno. She had a pretty high fever. I think she was out of her mind with it. Maybe it's something like the plague."

I wouldn't normally have come up with a theory like that, but I remembered hearing some customers talk about a few cases of it in a neighboring county.

"Or maybe it's drugs," Kate said. "I'm sure they'll do a tox screen at the hospital."

Somehow I didn't think it was drugs.

"I'm glad Ty told you to stay out of sight. Do you need anything? I'm coming down to get you guys."

"No," I said. "I'm okay."

"What are you thinking?" Kate said, after I was quiet for a minute.

"I'm wondering if something else happened to her tonight. Something worse."

"Worse, how?"

"The ghost that was haunting her. I'm wondering if he tried to kill her."

Chapter 30

In about half an hour, Kate and Ty arrived. I ran up to the car.

"How are you doing?" I asked, getting into the back seat.

He turned and nodded, but his eyes looked a little vacant.

"I need a hot shower and a pillow," he said yawning. "I talked to the cops but they still want me to come down to the station. I told them I would stop by in the morning. I don't know what else I can say. I already told them what happened."

"At least they didn't have you go in tonight," I said. "Did the press talk to you?"

"Oh, yeah," he said. "The guy was a real deep thinker. He seemed more interested in finding out how old I was than what happened. But it was no big deal. I just told him I swam out and brought her back. I kept it vague."

He eased his head back and closed his eyes while we drove. When we got to his house, I helped him out of the car, my arm around his waist as we walked slowly up to the door.

"She really flipped out, Abby. I keep thinking about it, remembering more. The things she was saying when I got to her. She was calling me all sorts of names. Things a crazy person would say."

"Like what?"

"I'd rather not repeat it, Abby. It was really ugly stuff."

An avalanche of dread rolled down inside me.

"And then she, I don't know. I guess she fainted. But the more I think about it, the more I'm not sure. I mean, it's all starting to feel like a dream."

I reached up and hugged him again, taking the keys from his hand and opening the door.

"It's been a long night," I said. "You need to get some rest."

But Ty seemed like he was still thinking about it.

"I think she was dead, Abby," he said. "She was dead in my arms as I swam with her back to shore. She was dead."

I had never seen him so shaken up before.

I took his hand and kissed it, my heart full and grateful that he was still here.

"Do you want me to stay with you tonight?" I asked.

He shook his head.

"No," he said. "I'm fine. Really. I'll call you in the morning."

"No," I said. "I'm staying. I'll just go tell Kate and I'll be right back."

He smiled and shuffled inside.

I helped him into the shower and went out to the kitchen. I looked in the refrigerator. There wasn't too much to work with. Beer and some empty take-out cartons. What used to be a hunk of cheese inside some foil. Some more beer. Three eggs. Just enough for an omelet I thought.

I found the salt and pepper in the cupboard along with some garlic powder and got down to work.

It was ready just as Ty came out of the shower. He was wearing some Hawaiian-style shorts and his hair was still wet.

"Better?" I said.

"Yeah." He sighed.

"Sit down. You must be starving."

He wolfed the omelet down in seconds without speaking like it was the best thing he had ever had.

I stared at his shirtless chest.

"Go ahead, get a good eyeful," he said. "Take a picture even, because it might be the last time you see me this way. You keep taking care of me like this and pretty soon there'll be a lot more of me to love."

He slapped his stomach and smiled wearily.

"Come on," I said. "Let's get you to bed."

***

He fell asleep almost before his head hit the pillow.

I lay there next to him, watching him breathe.

I thought about Paloma. I hadn't seen the ghost at the club or around her tonight. But I couldn't deny what I saw in her arms, inside her. There was a darkness there. A black energy, dark and thick and malevolent.

Paloma wasn't crazy. I was somehow sure of it now. But I didn't know what to do to help her.

It was 4:35 and I was still awake, the sky already lighting up, and the black feeling inside me grew with every passing minute. My mind jumped from Paloma to dark bodies of water waiting for victims. I thought about Ty in that water, how he could have just gone over the falls and could have been sucked away from me forever. I had come close to losing him, just like I had lost Jesse.

I thought about how it's easy to feel like everything in front of you will always be there, rock solid, but how in reality it's all just a terrible moment away from turning into dust.

I thought about Ty some more as I watched him sleep, about how brave he was to rescue someone he didn't even know. And that was just the point. Someone needed help, and without thinking, he was there.

That was Ty.

I would love him as hard and as strong and for as long as fate would allow. Before we disappeared into that darkness Bruce Springsteen sang about.

I love you, Ty. I love you.

Chapter 31

Ty's face was all over the local morning news. The TV report mainly focused on his daring rescue and didn't say much about Paloma, other than she was an unidentified woman in the river who fell in the water above the spillway.

He looked good on the screen. Even tired and wet, he was poised and confident as he spoke to the reporter, telling him what happened. They looped the footage all morning. *The Bugler* even offered their coverage for free on their online edition.

I went out before Ty woke up and brought back some donuts.

"Hey, hero," I said when he finally got up. "How are you doing?"

"I'm fine," he said. "I got some good sleep. I feel a lot better."

He smiled and seemed back to his usual self, his energy light and happy.

I handed him the white bag.

"You're trying to corrupt me," he said, as he inhaled the first one, powdered sugar flying in the air and on his shirt.

"I'm trying to keep you alive. You need to carb up after last night."

He put the last bite in his mouth as he grabbed his phone and keys.

"I'm walking over to get my car and then driving over to give my statement," he said.

I told him that I was going to try and see Paloma at the hospital.

"Wait for me," he said. "I want to come too."

"Okay, I'll just meet you back here."

Just over an hour later I drove us over to the hospital in his truck, placing the bouquet of sunflowers I had bought on Ty's lap.

"These are nice," he said. "Cheery."

"Yeah," I said. "I hope they help. How was it talking to the police?"

"Fine. Told them the same thing again. They say they're treating it like a suicide attempt. That's what all the witnesses are calling it. They asked me, but I said I didn't really know. I was just focused on getting her out of the river."

We crossed the highway, turned down Eighth, and weaved through the back streets over to the hospital.

Ty sighed.

"I just can't stop thinking about it, Abby," he said. "I keep seeing her desperate eyes and angry face in my mind."

I accelerated, making the light, and turning into the lot.

"She's messed up," I said. "I have to find a way to help her somehow."

"Maybe you can't. I don't know. This isn't up my alley, but she seemed so unstable out there. She needs professional help."

"Maybe," I said, not quite believing it.

I parked and we walked through the double doors of the hospital. I fought off the memories of the long nights I had

130

spent there after my drowning. I just wanted to think about Paloma now.

But they didn't let us see her. The nurse at the desk just shook her head.

"Sorry," she said. "No visitors."

"But this is the guy who saved her," I said.

She didn't look at Ty and kept her eyes on the chart.

"She's under observation. Only family can go in. But I can take those to her if you like."

I handed her the sunflowers.

"Tell her Abby and Ty were here," I said.

"Got it," she said, finally looking up. "I'm sure she appreciates everything you did for her."

We turned and walked back down the long corridor to the elevators, that hospital smell hanging in the air round us, almost making me gag.

"Wait," a voice said from behind us. "Wait!"

A woman ran up, dressed in scrubs and holding our flowers.

"Hi," she said, looking flustered and nervous. "I'm Paloma's sister, Rosie."

She looked a little like her but older, with small wrinkles around her puffy eyes.

"I'm Abby. Paloma told me you were a nurse. Nice to meet you. And this is Ty."

"Ty," she whispered.

Then she gave him a long hug, crushing the sunflowers between them.

"Thank you so much," she said, crying softly. "For pulling her from the river last night. I don't even know what else to say. Thank you seems so small compared to what you did."

She took his hand and held it.

"I'm so grateful that you were there. It was a miracle."

He smiled shyly and seemed a little embarrassed.

"I'm just glad she's okay," he said, looking over at me.

"How is she doing?" I asked.

She took a deep breath.

"She's okay," she said, lowering her voice. "She's very tired. She's been sleeping most of the time. She doesn't remember anything about last night. She doesn't even understand why she's in here. It just breaks my heart."

She started crying again.

"She'll be okay," Ty said, putting a hand on her shoulder. "She just needs a little time."

"I hope so," Rosie said. "She's been acting so crazy this last week. Not at all like herself. When they called me last night, I have to admit, part of me wasn't even surprised."

"Crazy?" I asked. "How?"

"Moody. Angry sometimes. Paloma's not like that. She's always been very outgoing and friendly. A lively spirit. Lots of friends and always out, having fun."

I nodded.

"Well," she said, looking back down the hall. "She'll be home tomorrow, if you want to stop by and see her. Or you can call me."

She reached in her pocket and handed me a card.

"I better get back. Thank you so much again, both of you." She took each of our hands and gave them a tight squeeze. "I don't know how to thank you, but when things settle down I'll think of something. God bless you. God bless you both."

Chapter 32

"So tell me again exactly what happened last night," David said as he sat down across from me. "And don't leave anything out."

I had already told him twice, but I didn't mind repeating it. It was all I could think about anyway, and it was nice to talk about it instead of having it stuck in my mind. Lyle was up at the register, but there was no line and not much to do. I was struggling to stay awake and thought about seeing if I could go home early.

I laid out the story once again, everything I could remember, even the part about how Paloma fainted in the water.

"I was right over at Velvet when all this was happening," David said. "Why didn't you text me? We would have come."

"It's not like it was a party," I said. "Anyway, tell me again what she said when she called you yesterday."

"She was adamant about finding you. I mean, now that I can put it into context, she was out of her mind I guess."

He stopped and was quiet for a moment.

"But she didn't even try calling me," I said. "And I know she has my number."

"See?" David said. "Cray cray."

"So you told her I was at Amber's?"

"Yeah. I told her you were at a party over there, at a house behind the store. So she found you, huh?"

"Yeah," I said.

I told him about her arms, how she had a fever, and how she just took off running.

"So do you think she's a total whack job or what?" he asked. "Or does this have to do with her ghost?"

"I don't know what to think. I have to talk to her, but they wouldn't let us see her at the hospital."

"Maybe Paloma just had too much to drink," he said. "Or drugs. Remember that weird cannibal story in Florida about the guy eating the other guy's face? Maybe it was like that."

"But Paloma wasn't trying to eat someone."

David broke out laughing.

"No, silly. They found marijuana in his system and they think he had a bad reaction to it."

"Maybe," I said.

"So how's Ty doing? Did he recover? I saw him on TV. He looked hot."

"Yeah, he's all good," I said.

"Abby Craig, between the two of you, it's like you're some superhero couple," he said as he stood up. "Going around saving people. They're going to have a movie about you two."

Lyle laughed.

"I'd go see that movie," he said.

"Oh, me too," David said, raising an eyebrow and walking away. "Me too."

***

I got a text from Kate asking if I could stop by the store on my way home from work.

I hated going into Safeway during the dinner hour. It was always crowded and full of exhausted, grumpy office workers. I grabbed a cart and weaved quickly down the aisle, throwing in items on my list. Milk, cereal, orange juice, bread.

I could hear Grace's voice on the store's intercom. She was one of the checkers I knew. She would always ask customers if they needed help to their cars. She would ask several times. It didn't matter how old or young they were or their physical condition or how many or how few groceries they had.

"And do you need help out with that today?"

She repeated it so often that sometimes it played over and over in my head for the rest of the day.

"And do you need help out with that today?"

I walked down the pasta aisle and it made me sad, thinking about how I used to have a lot of time for cooking. I missed it. I thought about the dinner party and how nothing had turned out right. I was looking forward to next month, when I would have more time. This fall would be my return to the kitchen. Until then, there wasn't time for anything other than Mondo pizza and pub burgers.

I turned down the next aisle and jumped, my heart almost stopping.

He was all the way down at the end, but I knew who it was. I couldn't see his face, but it looked just like him. He was even wearing that stupid Real Madrid soccer jersey he wore on the island.

It was Jack.

He was pretending to look at something on the shelf, but I knew better. He was waiting. Waiting for me.

I didn't stick around long enough to make sure it was him. I flew out of the store, leaving the shopping cart behind. Sweat collecting on my face. I rushed up to the

Jeep and started it, eyes glued to the front doors of the supermarket.

I sped away.

Chapter 33

I parked the Jeep a few blocks away from home. My breathing was still ragged and erratic. I closed my eyes for a minute and thought about what I had seen at the store. What I had really seen. Truthfully, I couldn't be sure it was Jack.

It didn't make sense. Why would he be back here, in plain sight, when the police were looking for him? Jack was nothing if not cunning and calculating. This would be the last place he'd be.

I talked myself down. I was tired from lack of sleep and all the recent excitement. That was all. I must have imagined it.

I turned the key in the ignition and drove back to the store.

***

I called Rosie the next afternoon during my break. Paloma had been released. She was at Rosie's. Her sister said that the doctors had given her some pretty strong sedatives and that she was still sleeping a lot. And that she probably would be for a while. I had asked if she needed anything and offered to stop by after work. But Rosie said no.

"I meant to ask you," I said. "Did they find anything in her system?"

I felt a little uncomfortable asking, but I had to know.

"You mean like drugs or alcohol?" she asked. "No. There was nothing, Abby."

"What did they say caused her fever?"

"Fever?" Rosie said. "She didn't have a fever. All her vital signs were normal."

She asked me if I could call back later that evening.

"It would be good for her to talk to a friend," she said. "I would invite you over, but I think we better wait until she's more rested."

I called Paloma before my soccer game, but there was no answer.

It was drizzling and a cool wind was blowing. I looked across the field and studied the team we were going to play. They had gotten new jerseys and had a new name, but I recognized them from last season. It was going to be a tough game.

Tim hit me with a perfectly timed pass, which I took in full stride, and after making a move around two defenders, I cut in and took a hard shot to the left of the keeper and into the back of the net. Sam scored the game-winning goal on a bending free kick in the second half.

I checked my messages after I said goodbye to the team.

Paloma hadn't called back.

***

I talked to Rosie again the next day. She said Paloma was feeling better. But when I called her a few times from home and Back Street, I still got no answer.

She was probably trying to work through everything that had happened. But I still had a lot of unanswered

138

questions and talking to her sister wasn't going to help me find out anything more about that ghost.

I needed to know what really happened that night in front of Amber's house and then in the river. Paloma might remember more now that some time had passed.

I figured that it was worth a shot. After my shift I drove over to Club 6. I thought that if she was feeling better, she might be back at work. It was just past seven, but the place was still closed. I knocked a few times anyway, hoping someone would answer.

"Not till nine," said a scruffy voice right before I was about to give up. A man wearing a ZZ Top tank top opened the door just a few inches, ready to close it again.

"Wait," I said. "I'm a friend of one of the dancers who works here. Paloma Suárez. Do you know if she's working tonight?"

"Pali's history," he said.

"What do you mean history?"

"She's done here, got it? She's missed three straight shifts without so much as a peep. I haven't heard squat. I can't have people working here who don't work here."

"You must be Eddie," I said.

He sighed and scratched the stubble on his chin and looked at me and then opened the door.

"Yeah, that's me. Come in for a minute," he said. "She left some of her stuff."

"Abby," I said, following him inside.

It was strange seeing the club so quiet. There were no blinding strobe lights or disco balls spinning, no scantily clad barmaids or people dancing in the middle of the room. It was just him and a television over the bar, tuned to a baseball game.

But even though it looked just like a regular room now, something about it didn't feel right.

We stopped at the bar and he faced me.

"So, you're a friend of hers, huh?" he asked.

I was getting a bad feeling, like we were being watched.

"Yeah."

His eyes were on me, checking me out.

"She's been going through a hard time," I said.

"Yeah, whatever. She can take a number. Anyway, she left one of her, uh, outfits here. Hold on, let me get it."

He left me standing there while he went into the back.

I wandered around a little, hoping that I could see something. But I didn't. There was nothing, then or now. Nothing except a feeling.

I saw ghosts all over town. I saw them rising up from rivers, in coffee shops, and at parks. It felt like there was something here. Why wasn't I seeing it? It didn't make any sense.

I looked around some more and then glanced up at the cage.

I jumped back.

It wasn't exactly a ghost, but there was something there just the same. Something I had never seen before. A dark mist was moving around inside the cage. It looked like black fog, and it was hovering behind the steel bars.

I blinked hard, my back glued to the wall. I was too scared to move.

I just stood there watching as mist moved around the cage. Suddenly it started spilling out, falling down onto the dance floor like a black waterfall.

Oozing and dripping, it slowly started to crawl toward me.

I held down a scream just as the owner came back out.

"Got it," he said. "Hey, you okay?"

I looked at him.

140

"Huh?"

I looked back over at the floor but the fog was gone, like it had never been there.

"Here," he said, handing me a bag. "I don't know, maybe you want to try it on. See if it fits."

I stared at him for a moment, not knowing what he meant.

"What are you talking about?" I said.

"Well, I'm short a girl now that Pali's gone. You don't exactly have her curves, but I think you might do. You might do just fine. I pay good and there's tips. What'd ya say?"

I gave him back the bag and walked away.

"Say, if you talk to her, tell her I'm really pissed," he yelled. "And think about the job offer."

I let the door slam hard behind me.

Chapter 34

"Mo!" I said as I walked in.

She looked up from behind the espresso machine and cracked a smile.

"Hey," she said, pulling a shot.

She was dressed in her usual tank top that showed off all her tattoos. Her hair was short and choppy and she had a small ring in her nose.

"How was your tour? How was Europe?"

"Sick," she said, nodding.

I slid my bag in the drawer.

"Are you guys playing a show here sometime?"

"Next week at The Horned Hand," she said.

"Cool. I'll be there," I said.

Mo was still the same. We didn't say much more the rest of the day, but it was nice having her back. The morning was smooth and lot of the regular customers treated her like a rock star. And even though she was still serious and quiet, I could tell she was pleased that so many people were happy to see her.

David showed up later and after talking to Mo for a good 15 minutes finally started helping me up front with the line.

"It's like our little family is all back together," he said as he walked by.

I sat in the crisp air outside on my break, the sun hitting my face but not helping much. I hadn't brought a jacket. But I didn't want to go back inside. It was too beautiful.

I still hadn't gotten ahold of Paloma. Even though Rosie had said she was doing better, I was still worried about her. I was also starting to feel a little resentment. I had reached out to her. Ty had pulled her out of the river. She could call me back. It wasn't too much to ask.

Lyle wandered out and handed me a small cup.

"Here, try this," he said, touching his afro. "It'll straighten your hair."

I took a sip.

"Wow," I said.

"Beans are from Hawaii. It's our newest blend. It's a bit more expensive, but it's my new favorite."

"Yeah," I said. "It's really smooth."

He went back inside as I eyed Kate's Subaru while she drove into the lot. I waved slowly as she got out of the car, surprised to see her.

She was wearing her new dark suit, the one she bought on her trip to Portland last month, and looked professional and serious. She walked over to me and sat down.

"Spiff," I said.

"Thanks," she said. She looked around at the customers sitting at the other tables and then smiled.

"Want some coffee? Lyle just brewed up our new blend. Here, try some."

She took a sip.

"This has a really nice flavor," she said. "I don't want any now, but can you bring a pound home?"

"Sure," I said.

There had to be a reason she was here.

"Looks like the tourist season finally tapered off. I can actually find a seat in this place now."

"Yeah, it's a little better," I said. "Hey, I thought you were busy all day. I wasn't expecting to see you."

"My interview got cancelled, so I thought I would stop by and say hi."

She stared out at the cars on the street, her energy moving fast around her.

"Plus I wanted to talk to you about something."

It was in the way she said it, those small pauses between the words, the slight breathlessness in her voice. Something was up. I sat back. A Jeep with a "Dog is my Co-Pilot" bumper sticker pulled up.

"So what's going on?" I said.

She rubbed her hands nervously and leaned close to me.

"It's good news, Abby," she said. "Really."

"Go ahead. I'm ready."

"It's about Jack Martin. They found him in Canada under an alias. Apparently, he's been there the entire time, living in Vancouver. He was arrested last night."

"What?" I said. "Are you sure? Are they sure it's him? I thought…"

"It's him," she said. "He's already in jail in Seattle. The FBI says they'll probably push the trial back now to early next year so they can include him. February, maybe March."

"I can't believe it," I said finally.

It was the news I had been dreaming about for months. Jack being caught and thrown in jail. He hadn't gotten away with it after all. He escaped off the island, but he hadn't gotten away.

"It's hard to believe," I repeated, still a little stunned.

I just sat there smiling, the breeze blowing back my hair.

Kate reached across the table and grabbed my hand.

"It's over, Abby," she said, tears in her eyes. "It's finally all over."

Chapter 35

The sun was still up when I walked through the door. Kate wasn't home yet. I got a soda and wandered outside to sit by the pond.

Since she had told me the news of his capture, I couldn't stop thinking about Jack Martin. And for once it was a good feeling, something else besides fear or anger. I was almost looking forward to the trial now. And I wanted the players on my soccer team to finally know what had really happened.

A strong wind scattered leaves on the grass and tried to knock down more from the trees above me as I called Ty to tell him the news.

"That's awesome, Abby," he said.

He was working and couldn't talk, but said he would call me later. As I said goodbye, a hummingbird floated down and stared at me, its long beak not far from my hand, and then zoomed away to the flowers by the fence.

But as I put the phone down, I remembered Jesse's warning. If it wasn't Jack around me, what was it? What had he seen?

I yawned and rubbed my eyes. It felt like I hadn't gotten any sleep in a long time. It felt like insomnia was creeping back into my life.

But now with Jack in jail, there would be time to catch up. I headed inside for a nap.

***

I woke up in the dark.

Country music in my ears, hot air blowing.

I sat up and looked around. The sound of a car engine rumbled through me, a road up ahead.

I was in a dream.

Riding in the back seat of a car.

All the windows were down, the air like fire on my face. My head throbbed as I stared out into the fierce night that stretched for miles and miles around us.

The motor shifted into another gear, and we picked up speed. Faster and faster down the highway. Too fast. The car then turned off onto a dirt road. It didn't slow down.

I stared up at the front seat, the driver finally coming into focus.

I could only see her hair, her eyes looking ahead in the mirror.

Short hair. Dark.

"Paloma!" I said. "Paloma, what's going on?"

But she didn't hear me. She just kept looking straight ahead as we drove on.

The music louder.

I started shaking.

"Paloma!" I shouted again. But suddenly, there was someone else driving.

I could only see the back of his head. Or what was left of it. Then I saw his reflection in the rearview mirror. His eyes seemed to glow. And something else.

The hot air pouring into the car had pushed back his hair. There was a hole in his forehead. A bullet hole.

He started to laugh. My head ached, pounding to the beat of the music on the radio. I tried to scream, but nothing came out. Fear and rage and adrenaline coursed through me as I tried to move. But I couldn't.

I looked up again at the mirror and caught his eyes staring at me. He saw me.

He saw me.

"You're next," he said, his voice low and gravelly.

He began laughing again. The car was moving faster, jumping higher and higher in the air with every rise and dip of the rough road. It was losing control.

Then I felt it bounce off the road and fly through the air. I could see a large boulder illuminated in the headlights. We were heading straight for it.

"Paloma!" I shouted. "Paloma!"

My screams were drowned out by the sound of metal hitting rock.

Everything went black.

***

I woke up screaming, drenched in sweat.

I sat up and grabbed the glass of water from the nightstand.

I drank it down, staring at the curtains blowing. It was dark outside. I was hot, so very hot. I went over to the window and felt the cool breeze against my face. It wasn't a dream. I was sure of it. I could still hear his laughter.

I made it to the bathroom just as the vomit came up.

Chapter 36

I was sitting on the sofa, trying to calm down when something exploded up above the house. I jumped.

I walked over to the window and slid open the curtains. It looked like the huge storm that had been threatening most of the summer had finally arrived. Hard, heavy drops spit down from the sky, pounding the pavement out in front of the house. Another quick, sudden flash lit everything up, followed by another loud crash. A moment later thunder shook the house again.

My phone rang.

I looked at it and didn't recognize the number.

I glanced out at the storm, not remembering if it was dangerous to talk on a cell phone while the skies were still crackling overhead with electricity. But something told me that I needed to answer this call.

"Hello?"

"Uh, is this Abby?" the woman's voice said. She sounded familiar, but I couldn't quite place from where.

"Yeah, this is me."

"Hi, Abby. It's Rosie. Rosie Suárez."

I walked back over to the window as another large crack of thunder shattered overhead.

"Have you heard from Paloma?" she asked. "She's not there with you, is she?"

"No," I said, the dread building inside me. "I haven't heard or seen her since the river. Why?"

Rosie was quiet for a moment. I heard a loud boom on the line.

"She's gone, Abby," she said. "When I got home from work, she wasn't here. I knew something was wrong when I went over to her apartment during my lunch break to pick up some things for her, you know clothes and some of her things. But her car wasn't there. And then when I came home she was gone, Abby. But her phone was still here. She never goes anywhere without her phone. I've been calling her friends and no one's seen her. I don't know where she could be. I have a really bad feeling."

She was rambling and crying now.

I didn't want to tell her I had the same exact feeling.

I could feel the bile coming up my throat. It sounded like the vision. Paloma was out there somewhere. Driving. Out there with *him*. I fought off the overwhelming sense that we were too late.

"Have you, uh, checked the hospitals?" I said, hating to ask.

"No," she said. "*Dios mío*. Please, God, no."

"Rosie, she could be a lot of places. Let's take it one step at a time. You check the hospitals and I'll try to find out what I can. We'll find her, Rosie. We'll find her."

Before hanging up we agreed to call each other back with updates.

I knew that if he had the power to kill her, he would. I just prayed he wasn't strong enough yet.

I went over to the door and opened it, watching the broken flower pots fill up with hail.

Paloma was somewhere out there in the storm.

Chapter 37

I knew I had to find Jesse. The evil haunting Paloma must have been the darkness he had sensed around me. I wasn't sure what he could do, if he could help me find her. But I had to try. I didn't know where else to turn.

It was just past nine when I got to the park.

The hail had stopped but it was still raining hard. Thunder boomed overhead.

"Jesse," I whispered as I walked through the deluge.

The park was deserted. I followed the lighted path over to the basketball court.

"Jesse, please, I need to talk to you."

His words screamed in my head as I circled the park twice in the hard rain. How he had been having trouble finding me and how it might not be up to him when he had to leave. And that maybe he couldn't get back to me.

I hoped to see a tall figure wearing a baseball cap, standing somewhere, anywhere.

But I didn't.

"Jesse! Please, Jesse."

The more I called in vain, the more I was gripped by the almost certain knowledge that he was Paloma's only chance.

"I have to talk to you."

Nothing.

He wasn't there.

He wasn't anywhere.

It was hopeless. Completely hopeless.

I turned to head back to the parking lot.

And that's when I saw him.

He was standing in the shadows, by the river, staring at me.

His eyes were glowing.

I shuddered.

A black, ominous mist floated around him as he started moving toward me.

I could see his face now. The hair was back down over his forehead. I couldn't see the bullet hole. But I knew it was there.

The ghost of Clyde Tidwell kept coming closer and closer, his horrible eyes burning brighter and brighter with an evil I wouldn't have believed possible.

Staring.

Coming for me.

Closer.

Closer.

I backed away, trying to break free from his spell.

"Run," I heard someone scream in my head. "Run!"

I found my legs and sprinted as fast as I ever had in my life, hearing the sound of his laughter all the way back to the Jeep.

Chapter 38

The meat and potatoes and carrots and onions had come together.

I lifted the lid, the sweet aroma of the stew filling my nostrils. I took a taste.

That's right.

I gave it another stir and then chopped the fresh parsley I had picked from the garden. It was torture having to wait while everything simmered, the vegetables giving themselves over to the beef.

The heat from the oven made me sweat. I wiped the moisture off my forehead, took the biscuits out, flaky and golden.

That's right.

Kate walked in.

"Abby," she said. "What are you doing here? And what's that?"

I followed her finger to where she was pointing.

"Dutch oven, sis," I said. "Cooking food how it's meant to be cooked. I picked it up today while I was out. Hey, dinner in ten minutes. Hope you're hungry!"

She gave me a strange look and then left. I poured the whiskey. Then I ladled the stew into bowls. I lovingly slid the biscuits onto a plate. It was time to eat.

Kate walked back out and gave me a hug. Boy, did she smell divine. Like flowers in the rain. I handed her a drink and raised my glass.

"Now don't get roostered," I said.

"What?" Kate said, smelling the whiskey and then looking at me. "I guess you've been hanging around David a little too much."

I just smiled, laughing a little.

She dug in, just like I was hoping. She needed to put a little flesh on her bones.

We sat there eating, the flavors sharp, so sharp on my tongue.

"This is delicious," I said with food still in my mouth.

"Is Ty coming over?" she asked.

"Ty?"

"Yeah, is he coming or is he working tonight?"

I paused, trying to think. My mind was sluggish. All day, it had been so sluggish.

"Working," I said finally, with authority.

I had a headache.

"Well, thanks for making dinner. It's, ah, good. Have you heard from Paloma yet?"

I shrugged.

"No," I said. "Well, yes, in a manner of speaking."

There it was again.

She was giving me another strange look.

I played with the food in front of me. My stomach suddenly didn't feel right and my head was aching now.

"More?" I asked.

"No, thanks. Abby, are you okay? Did something happen at work?"

She moved closer to me, studying my eyes, the expression on her face growing stranger.

"Work?" I said.

"Yeah. Work. You had an early shift, right?"

"No," I said, holding my head in my hands. "Day off. It feels like I haven't slept in a long time. A real long time."

"Why don't you go take a nap? You don't look so good. Go on. I'll see you for a movie later."

I went to my bed and fell into a deep, deep sleep.

Chapter 39

I didn't open my eyes until morning, the light dancing with the shadows from the leaves on the floor of my bedroom, the birds chirping.

I sat up. It was just after eight. I had slept through the entire night.

"Here she is," Kate said, walking in and handing me her phone. "It's Ty. He said your phone isn't working."

"Hey," I said to both of them at the same time.

"What happened to you yesterday?" he said.

"Sorry. I fell asleep. Did we have plans?"

"Well, not really, but it felt like I haven't seen you in a long time. So I stopped by after work, but you were lights out. You're just getting up now? You feeling okay?"

"Yeah. I feel, I don't know, really rested. I hope you weren't worried or anything."

"No," he said. "I just wanted to see you. Hey, have you heard from Paloma yet?"

I suddenly remembered. The dream. Paloma. The park. I was supposed to check in with Rosie. I wondered if she had learned anything.

"No," I said. "Listen, can I call you back?"

I hung up without waiting for him to answer.

Kate came back and took her phone.

"Okay, Abby, I gotta get going."

She moved closer and studied my face.

"You look better. I'm glad you got some good sleep."

She started to leave but then stopped.

"Oh, hey, I didn't get a chance to clean up last night. See what you can do. Looks like you were planning another dinner party or something."

"What? Sure."

"See you later, Abby."

A few seconds later I heard the front door close.

I picked up my phone. It was out of juice. I plugged it in. I would have to call Rosie from work.

I got up and took a shower. I got dressed, put on a little makeup, and headed out to make some coffee.

My mouth dropped open as I stood in the doorway, staring at the kitchen.

Every cookbook in the pantry was out across the granite counter. All 22 of them, my entire collection. All opened to recipes with the corners folded over, black illegible scribbles from a fat marker on the pages.

This is what Kate was talking about. She thought I was planning another dinner party.

She thought I had done this.

But it wasn't me.

Chapter 40

I didn't want to scare Kate, but she had to know about the break in. I tried to text her but the message wouldn't go through. I knew she was busy all morning. I would try her again later.

Someone must have broken in. It was the only possible answer.

It must be connected to what Jesse had been talking about.

Someone was after me, and they had broken into the house last night.

I shivered at the thought as I drove to work. Jack Martin was locked up, but maybe there were more. Maybe there were others who wanted to continue Nathaniel Mortimer's experiments.

I walked in and said hello to Lyle who was at the register with a customer. He gave me an odd look.

"Hi, Abby," he said finally. "Are you all right?"

"Yeah," I said, a little flustered. "I'll be up here in a minute."

I put on my apron as Mike came up, scratching at his beard.

"So, ah, Abby," he said. "What happened to you yesterday?"

"Happened? What do you mean?"

"You never showed up for your shift. You didn't call in or anything. We left a bunch of messages."

I shook my head.

"I was here yesterday. Remember? I stocked the storeroom and did inventory. I signed in and everything. I was working with Lyle."

Lyle was eavesdropping and walked over.

"No," he said. "That was the day before. I wasn't even working yesterday."

"What? No, that was yesterday."

"Lyle, can you help the next customer?" Mike said.

I followed Mike into the back where he shuffled through papers and handed me the timesheet. I searched for my name, relieved when I found it. I showed him.

"Abby," Mike said. "That was for Wednesday."

"Yeah. Yesterday. I was here."

"No. It's Friday today. Yesterday, on Thursday, you never showed up for your shift."

As I stared at the paper, his words sank in.

"So, today is Friday?" I asked slowly.

He nodded.

What was I doing yesterday? I couldn't remember. Everything was fuzzy.

"Mike, I'm so sorry," I said. "I must have just gotten mixed up. I wasn't thinking, I guess."

"That's okay," he said, rubbing his beard again. "It happens. No worries. Mo came in and covered for you. Mostly, we were worried 'cause we couldn't reach you. I'm glad you're okay."

"Yeah. Sorry again. I really don't know what happened."

***

During my break I tried to check my messages, but there was something wrong with my phone. It had power and I could see that I had several messages, but I couldn't access them. My fingers felt strange. Puffy or something.

"I just don't understand it," I said to Mike later.

"It's okay, Abby," he said. "Really, it's no big deal."

When Mo came in, I thanked her for covering for me.

"Sorry, I just spaced out."

"Been there," she said.

David showed up for the last two hours of my shift. I was happy to see him.

I told him about Paloma being gone.

"I'll make a few calls," he said. "Maybe some of my peeps have seen her."

I thought that almost 24 hours had passed since Rosie had seen her last. She would probably be able to file a missing persons report. Whatever good that would do.

I had to try to find Jesse again.

It had felt like only a few minutes had passed since I started my shift. But the clock didn't lie. It was time to go home.

I walked through the door and took out my phone. It still wasn't working.

David was out in front on a break.

"I'll call you later if I hear anything," he said. "Oh, and I wouldn't dream of telling you what to do, but if I did I would tell you that you better apologize to Mo when you see her. Or give her a call tonight. Girlfriend was pissed off and you don't want her stewing, believe you me."

"What do you mean apologize?" I said, stopping and looking at him. "I already thanked her for covering for me yesterday."

"No, not that," he said. "Something you said to her earlier while you guys were in the back."

"But I was never even in the back," I said. "I was out helping customers all day."

David's face broke out in a huge grin.

"Boy, someone needs to get home and get some rest, Abby Craig," he said. "You were back there doing inventory for like hours. Mo said she went to help out and you went all Miami Cannibal on her and chewed her head off. Called her a bunch of names. She was steamed."

I still didn't know what he was talking about. I shook my head and walked to the parking lot.

I drove down the street, thinking what a strange day it had been. It started raining again. My stomach was suddenly woozy. I stopped the Jeep and kicked open the door and then threw up in the street.

"What's going on?" I whispered, bent over in the rain.

I wiped my mouth with the back of my hand and rubbed my face on my sleeve, the stench of vomit all around.

Chapter 41

I walked into the house, my head pounding.

"Abby, where have you been? Ty called. He's looking for you."

I walked past Kate and stared at the television.

"You're all wet. Have you been out in the rain? Are you okay?"

She reached over and put her icy hand on my head.

"Oh, my God, you're burning up," she said. "Abby, you're sick. I'll be right back. I'm getting the thermometer."

"I'm fine," I said to her back.

I heard heavy rain on the roof, the sound of it tearing through my skull. I sat on the sofa, but slipped off the leather onto the floor.

"I'm fine, I'm fine," was the last thing I remembered saying.

***

Ty pulled me closer.

"You'll be okay," he said.

An old movie was playing in the background. I put my ear to his chest and listened to his heartbeat. I felt safe.

"This is the best I've felt all day," I said.

I could hear the rain still, on the rooftop, on the window.

"Here, put this blanket around you. You're shaking."

"I think she's dead. I don't think she could survive him. He's too powerful. She's out there dead somewhere."

"Shhh," Ty said. "Just rest. I'll be back in the morning."

I was in bed suddenly, darkness around me.

I was hot.

So hot.

Like I was in hell.

Chapter 42

I sat up, dizzy, my stomach nauseous again, my throat hurting. My head burning.

"Kate?" I whispered.

I was in bed and I must have been sleeping for hours, since getting home. I was in my pajamas, the volume from the small TV low.

"Kate?" I said again, throwing the covers off.

I was soaked in sweat. I heard her slippers on the wood floor.

"Abby, you're up," she said, pushing pillows behind me. "How are you feeling?"

Her eyes were wide and crazy, studying me.

"Like shit on a stick," I said. "I guess I have the flu."

"Such a mouth," Ty said and smiled, taking my hand.

"You're here," I said.

"Of course. Kate called me and I came over after work."

"What time is it?"

"Almost midnight," he said. "Do you need anything? I'm going to the store."

"No," I said.

"Get some rest and I'll see you in a little while," he said, kissing my forehead. "I love you, Abby. Try and feel better."

***

"Your temperature was up to 103. But you're cooler now."

I nodded.

"That's a good sign," she said. "Can I get you anything?"

I shook my head.

"Here. Drink some water," she said. "And then I'll help you change."

I sat up, letting her guide my arms and legs into shorts and a T-shirt. I started coughing and shivering as I laid back down while Kate pulled heavy covers over me.

I couldn't think straight, big black holes in the middle of my thoughts with everything spinning like I was on one of those rides at a fair. Up, up, up in the air, spinning and lost in the sky, spinning and lost.

Spinning.

My arms and legs ached. It felt like I had been running for days. Weeks. My whole life.

Chapter 43

I woke up with mud on my feet and rain on my face. I was shivering, standing outside. Lost.

"No! Abby!" she yelled, her words echoing in my ears over and over again. "Don't do it! Put down the shovel! Put it down!"

I shook my head. Kate was standing in front of me, horror in her eyes. We stood in the rain.

"Kate?" I screamed. "What's the matter? Why are we outside?"

But she didn't answer me.

"Abby," she said again. "Abby, put the shovel down. Drop it. Now!"

What was she talking about? But then I followed my arms up to my hands and saw it.

"Just put it down," she repeated.

We were standing in the backyard, the rain coming down in sheets. I didn't want to let it go, didn't want to let it fall from my hands.

I inhaled, looked up, and let the rain hit my face.

And threw it down behind me.

"Good," she said. "Now, take my hand."

We stumbled to the house, like we were drunk. I bent over and threw up in the mud.

"Come on, Abby," she yelled again. "You need to get inside."

I just stood there. I couldn't feel my feet or my hands. I couldn't feel anything. I tried to breathe, but couldn't, couldn't move. The light from the porch burned into my eyes, the smell of mud strong in my nostrils.

Kate was holding a gun.

"You can't shoot me anymore!" I heard someone shout.

"What are you saying, Abby?" she said, putting it in her pocket. "Take it easy."

"Leave me alone," I said as she dragged me over the grass, through the kitchen, down the hallway. "Leave me alone. Get your filthy hands off of me, whore!"

**

I crept to the bathroom and turned on the faucet, letting the cold water run over my hands and splashing some of its cool sweetness on my face, on my neck, in my hair.

"Better," I said in a low voice. "Much, much better."

I looked in the mirror.

Those stark eyes, the scar running down my face, the mustache.

Handsome as ever.

**

I opened my eyes and didn't recognize where I was.

The dark hallway smelled of coffin varnish, as though the wooden floors had been soaking the whiskey up for decades upon decades. The strong smell of tobacco lingered in the air, along with the stench of sweat. And other bodily fluids.

I stood in the shadows, waiting for someone.

The sound of laughing and yelling erupted from down-stairs, drowning out the piano music for a few moments.

I felt different. Strong, like my hands could crush what-ever they came in contact with. Like I could bend whatever was between my hands to my liking. As if they were made out of iron.

I heard her coming up the stairs, her heels heavy and leaden against the wooden steps.

The sight of her made the blood in my veins turn to liq-uid fire. An anger more intense than I'd ever known rushed through me.

But it wasn't uncontrollable anger. It was a perfect rage. I was in charge of it. Completely. It bent to my will.

She walked past me, her long lace dress dragging on the floor. She was alone. She didn't see me.

As she opened the door to her room, I lunged out of the shadows and took her by the arm, squeezing it with my grip of pure iron.

"I know you've been holding out on me, Inez," I said, tightening my fingers.

She screamed and looked at me with desperate, animal eyes. The terror made me smile. Her eyes pleaded for a mercy that would never come.

"No," she blubbered. "I promise you. I wouldn't do that to you, Clyde. You take care of me."

"Where's the money, whore?" I said, pushing her into the room.

She cried out and collapsed down on the floor.

"Why would I do that to you? You let me stay here in your hotel. Why would I keep money from you?"

"Don't lie to me, slut," I said, the anger growing stronger.

"I'm not," she sobbed. "I'm telling you the truth."

But I knew she was lying. She was like all the rest. Cutting corners and sloppily planning their great escapes. Trying to steal what was mine and make a fool of me. Trying to rob me behind my back.

I wouldn't stand for it. My iron hands were the instrument of my justice.

I grabbed her and made her stand up.

Soon, they were around her, squeezing tighter and tighter. Her large brown eyes bulged out of their sockets. I wanted to hold a mirror up to them so they could see what she had brought upon herself. I wanted those eyes to witness the wrong of what she'd done. I wanted her to know. I wanted her to pay.

And she did.

She fought for breath, but she was weak. She was like a newborn calf in my hands. My terrible iron hands. She was weak and feeble and worthless.

In a few moments, the light went out of those eyes, and I let her limp body drop to the floor.

She understood now. I had made her see the error of her ways.

My hands felt alive. I felt alive, power pumping through my veins like a train from hell ripping through the night.

I looked at her dead body, and I looked back at my hands.

And sure as she was lying there, I knew there would be more.

I never wanted to feel anything else.

***

Kate was crying.

"What happened?"

"Rest now, Abby. I'm right here. I'll be here with you all night. Hang in there."

I saw a man in the corner and I screamed.

"Kate," I yelled. "It's him! It's the ghost of Clyde Tidwell. The one who killed Paloma!"

I screamed again with everything I had, thrashing my arms and legs on the bed. My face hurt, thick drool leaking out of my mouth.

"Get him out of here," I yelled.

But she wouldn't listen. She let him move closer to her.

"No, Kate! No! Stay away from him."

Then the ghost turned into someone else.

"Shhh, Abby," Dr. Krowe said, staring down at me, a stethoscope in his ears and on my chest. "You'll be okay."

I was so hot. Burning, burning, burning.

I pushed him away, pushed him away from me.

"I'm just here to help," he said.

"Here to help?" I heard myself screaming. "Here to help? Help yourself. Help *yourself*."

I fell back into the strange darkness, repeating those words over and over again and laughing so hard it hurt my face.

Chapter 44

It was the deepest blue sky I had ever seen.

I threw myself down on the ground, staring up at it, swimming and dancing in the rich color.

"I can see it!" I screamed. "I can see it, Jesse! I can see colors again!"

"Of course you can, Craigers," Jesse said, taking my hand. "They were here the whole time."

I turned and looked at him, hearing the tears fall off my face, like rain, hitting the ground in a loud splash.

"Oh, Jesse," I said. "Your eyes are the most incredible green. I've missed them so much. They look like emeralds. And the grass. The leaves. They're so beautiful. This is so amazing."

I sat up and looked around. We were in a field, the sun bright, the blue sky laid out in front of us like those long, lost summers of our childhood. I looked at my shirt. Purple. My shoes were white with yellow streaks on the sides.

"It's a miracle. I can see color again. Everything is so deep and rich. Where are we?"

He sighed.

"Somewhere you don't belong," he said.

I touched his cheek.

"It's okay," I said. "It's all good."

"No," he said. "It's not. It's not good. Look."

He pointed. Way in the distance, someone was walking.

"But I'm going to try. I'm going to try and help you."

"I love you," I said, rolling over and hugging him. "I love you so much, Jesse."

Then I looked back up at the black shadow figure now walking quickly toward us, still just a silhouette against the sunlight. And then I saw those eyes. Those terrible, stark, light blue eyes.

Sharp as obsidian.

He was coming right for us, crossing the grass.

Jesse pulled me up. I squinted in the sunlight, staring.

He was getting closer and closer.

"He's growing off of your energy," Jesse said. "I have to stop him."

"Don't go," I yelled. "Jesse. Don't leave me again. I love you!"

"Run, Craigers!" he said, letting go of my hand. "Stay away from him. Now. Run!"

Clouds came in and the rain started, my feet stuck, sinking in the mud that was suddenly everywhere. I stared at Jesse, who was going full speed, flying into it, while his voice was still in my ears, screaming at me to run.

I ran toward the light. With Jesse's words still echoing in my head, I ran through the colors and left them behind.

His voice fell away as his world disappeared behind me.

Chapter 45

The sunlight was in my face. Kate was sitting on the bed, looking at me.

"How are you feeling?" she said.

I reached up and touched my head. My stomach felt okay finally. I didn't feel hot anymore.

"Better," I said.

She reached over and felt my head and nodded.

"You're a lot cooler."

I looked around. Ty wasn't in the room.

"Where's Ty?" I asked. "I thought he was coming back."

Her eyes fell to the floor.

"He was here for a long time. You've been pretty out of it for two days."

"Two days? That can't be."

"I told him to go home and get some rest."

"Tell him I want to see him," I said. "If he calls. Tell him to come back."

She didn't answer right away.

"Just rest. Rest, Abby. You're improving. That's all that matters at this point. You're okay now. You're safe."

***

The water felt warm on my skin and I stood in the shower for a long time and let it wash the dried sweat and grime away. When I came out, I felt new again. Stronger.

The dream and Jesse were still vivid in my mind. The colors, Jesse, the black figure walking toward me. Was it just a dream? I didn't know what any of it meant, but it felt like it had happened, that he ran off to fight the darkness that was coming for me.

I had to find him. And make sure he was okay.

I went out to the kitchen and sat down at the table. Kate put down toast, some grapes, and a glass of orange juice in front of me.

"Let's see how that sits before you eat a real meal."

I was wearing a purple shirt in the vision. And I saw it. I saw the color.

Kate sat across from me with large eyes. I kept eating until everything was gone.

"It's good to see you eat," she said, smiling weakly. "It's been days."

"That's how it feels," I said, wiping my mouth. "Now tell me what you're not telling me."

Chapter 46

We moved to the living room and I pulled a fleece blanket around me and put my feet up on the coffee table. Kate sat down, close to me, tucking the blanket under my legs.

"The important thing is that you're all right now. We were so worried about you. You were really sick. Coughing and throwing up a river. You had a high fever. You said some really crazy things. That's why I called Dr. Krowe. He was here, do you remember?"

"Yeah," I said. "I think so."

"Even he was shocked at some of the things coming out of your mouth. He said it was the fever making you say them."

"I think it was the same thing as Paloma," I said. "The ghost was trying to get in me, too."

"Not trying, Abby. He *was* in you. You weren't yourself. You weren't right in the head."

The hairs on the back of my neck stood up.

"And it wasn't just what you were saying. You were sleepwalking too. You went in the back yard and dug up all the flowers."

"What?"

She didn't look at me, just nodded.

"I brought you back inside," she said, her voice cracking.

I didn't remember any of it.

"It's true," she said, clearing her throat. "But it all still gives me chills. When I asked you what you were doing, you looked at me with these crazy eyes and told me that you were digging my grave."

I started shaking.

"Oh, my God, Kate," I said. "I'm so sorry. I'm so, so sorry."

"It wasn't you, Abby," she said, hugging me. "I know it wasn't you."

"I don't remember any of it. None of it."

"I know," she said. "It's lucky that you don't."

We were quiet for a minute.

"What happened to Ty?" I said, almost afraid to ask. I could feel something wasn't right.

"He was here," she said. "For most of it. But last night, you were delirious, screaming and yelling."

"I scared him off?" I said.

"I don't know," she said. "But you kept calling out for Jesse."

I remembered that.

"What else? Tell me."

"You said that you loved him," she said. "You said you loved Jesse."

"Damn it. God damn it."

I felt like crying and held my head in my hands. I told Kate about the dream with Jesse and how something was after us, a dark energy with these bright blue eyes.

"I saw the color, Kate," I said. "I saw them."

"Your eyes were blue some of the time," she said. "Light blue. It was freaking me out."

"Jesse fought it. He told me to run while he fought the demon. I don't know if he made it. I have a bad, bad feeling about it."

But then I thought back to Ty.

"Has he called?"

"Of course," she said. "About a thousand times. You'll see him soon. Ty can handle it. Give him some time."

I nodded, sitting quiet for a moment.

"God damn it," I repeated.

Chapter 47

"What about Paloma?" I asked, dreading what Kate would say. "Have you heard anything?"

"It's good news, Abby," she said. "She's okay."

Kate told me that Paloma had been found wandering around on a forest road somewhere outside of Prineville. She had driven her car deep into the wilderness and crashed into a boulder. She had suffered a concussion and a broken collarbone.

"It seems like she blacked out for a while. When she came to, she waited for help to come," Kate said. "But when she realized no one knew where she was and that she seemed to be out in the middle of nowhere, she started following the car tracks back.

"Some hunters found her and drove her to the hospital. They checked her out and the doctors said she's fine. She went home yesterday. One of the first things she did was call you."

"That's great news," I said. "I'm so relieved."

"There was something, though, that the doctors couldn't explain," Kate said. "Paloma had a lot of cuts and bruises from the accident. But there were some bruises around her neck that weren't consistent with a car accident. Off the record, one of them told me that it looked like someone had tried to choke her."

Chapter 48

The sun was low in the cloudy October sky, the air smelled of wet leaves and burning wood stoves. I slid on my FC Barcelona track jacket and stepped outside, walking past Mo sitting on the curb, sucking down smoke.

I stared at the new tattoo on her leg. It was of a gargoyle with a tongue sticking out. Underneath it the word "Paris" was written in large cursive letters.

"You closing tonight?" I asked her.

She stomped out the butt on the cement and stood up.

"Yeah," she said.

"Have a good one," I said. "See you tomorrow."

"Later," she said.

Kate had insisted I take some time off, convinced that I had been working too many hours all summer and that it had contributed to what had happened. It was my first day back in a week. Kate never referred to it as a possession, but as an illness. I didn't know what it had been, I just knew that it was great to be alive.

Apologizing to Mo was the first thing I did when I came back. I didn't know what I said, so when I found her in the storage room, I was honest.

"Mo, look, I'm sorry. Sorry for what I said to you even though I don't remember any of it."

"You called me a slut, you bitch," she said.

Just hearing the words rattled me.

"I was sick," I said. "I called my sister worse from what I hear."

She waved me off like she had already let it go.

Like I did every day, I drove to the park and looked for Jesse.

I couldn't find him to thank him for what he did, for battling that *thing* on the field.

He wasn't around.

I couldn't feel him anywhere.

I called out to him. I begged him to come back.

But I knew.

The darkness that had tried to take me had succeeded in taking him.

Jesse was gone.

And this time it was forever.

Chapter 49

In the end I loved them both and lost them both.

I hadn't seen Ty in weeks and I ached to be in his arms again.

We had talked a few times on the phone about what had happened, but it didn't help any. I was up front about everything. The evil ghost, seeing Jesse in a dream, seeing Paloma in my vision. It was who I was now, and I was hoping Ty would accept it.

I knew it was a lot to take on and as the days went by and I didn't hear from him, I wondered if it was all too much.

"Be patient with me, Abby," he had said sadly one day. "I just need a little time to sort all this out."

I tried.

A week slipped away. And then two.

He finally called on a Wednesday afternoon. I heard his voice and cried. I needed to see him, hold him. Kiss him.

We met along the river, soggy leaves under our feet.

"I didn't know if you were really going to come," I said as he walked up to me. His energy was darker than usual even though he smiled.

He kissed me and then took my hand, giving me hope.

"Of course I'd come," he said.

He wiped a tear off my cheek and we walked quietly for a few minutes, crossing the footbridge and sitting on an empty bench.

"I know I hurt you," I said. "Saying those things about Jesse. But I love you, Ty. You're the one. You're the one I want to be with. I love you with all my heart."

He looked away. Didn't say anything.

"Is it because of what happened during the fever?" I said finally.

"That's part of it. But I'm so glad and relieved you're okay, Abby."

He paused.

"It's just that it's made me realize that this whole other world between us is so big. I don't understand it, and that's okay as long as there's nothing too serious going on. But this. This made me realize that you see something that I'll never see. You're part of something I can't ever be part of."

I nodded.

"And I see that it's between us now. You said that a long time ago. And I thought it wasn't such a big deal, but I was naive. I didn't understand. I didn't understand any of it."

I looked away.

"I thought it would be okay," he said. "That we would be okay. But now, honestly, I'm not sure."

He brought my hand to his lips and kissed it softly. His eyes looked so sad and lost.

"That and I think I realized too that Jesse is really your Perseus. He's the one who saves you. And he's the one you really love."

"But that's just not true," I said, desperately. "That's not true, Ty. I love you."

I couldn't lose him.

"I love you," I said again.

"I can't feel this way. It hurts too much. I have to figure it out on my own. It has to make sense before we can go on."

Tears spilled down my face.

Then he said it.

"If we can go on."

I tried to stop crying, tried to be strong. We walked along the river for a long time afterwards as the light faded in the trees ripe in their autumn.

He then took my hand as leaves fluttered down, floating around us like butterflies.

Chapter 50

A light film of sparkling frost covered the gray track.

I zipped up my North Face jacket tight around me. The evenings were becoming more and more chilly, leaving behind crystal-covered reminders that winter was coming. The first snow of the season couldn't be far away.

But on this particular morning the sun was still making its presence felt, quickly melting the frost. I made my way gingerly around the oval, doing my best to avoid any lingering patches of ice.

It had taken Paloma and me time to recover from the psychic and physical abuse we suffered at the hands of Clyde Tidwell. We spoke on the phone a few times but whenever we tried to meet something always came up.

After a few laps, I spotted her sitting on the bench. The same bench where she had told me about him in what felt like a lifetime ago.

I walked over. I was strangely nervous, but I didn't exactly know why.

She looked up and waved at me.

"Hi, Abby," she said, a bright smile dancing on her lips. "It's so good to see you, girl."

"Hey, Pal o' mine," I said. "It's been too long."

She stood up and gave me a giant bear hug, like I was a friend she hadn't seen in a long, long time. There was a lightness in her face that I had never seen before. Like a great weight had been lifted off her chest and she could breathe again. She looked young and happy, nothing like the way she looked the last time I had seen her after she had tried to drown herself.

"You look like you're feeling better," I said.

"I am," she said. "Better than I have in a long time. I feel like I used to before all of this happened."

"I'm really glad."

She paused for a moment. She suddenly seemed nervous. Then she let out a sigh.

"I wanted to thank you, Abby. For how you helped me."

I shook my head.

"I didn't do anything, Paloma. I wish I could have done more, done something, but I was pretty useless. I'm not the one you should be thanking. It wasn't me."

I thought of Jesse. He should be the one she was thanking. Jesse was the one who had stopped Clyde Tidwell. Jesse was the one who had freed both of us from his power.

"You're wrong," she said. "You believed in me and you did what you could. You helped me a lot more than anyone else."

I was silent. I still didn't think I was worthy of her gratitude, but I didn't want to argue with her.

"He was a bad man," she said, watching a runner with a dog pass the "No Pets Allowed" sign. "When he... when he was controlling me, I saw some of what he did to those women. It was..."

She sighed again and rubbed her face.

"I know," I said. "I saw it, too."

She looked over at me.

"You too?"

I nodded slowly.

"It was horrible," I said. "I'm so sorry that happened to you, Paloma. But he's gone now. He won't hurt you again."

"How do you know that?" she said. "How can you be so sure?"

I let out a long breath.

"I just know," I said. "I had a friend who got rid of him."

She looked at me for a moment and then stared off in the distance. I could tell there was more she wanted to ask, but she had the good sense not to.

I couldn't talk about Jesse with her just now. What he had done for me, for us, and what he had sacrificed was just too painful to face right now. It was still too fresh. Maybe someday I would tell her. But not today.

"Hey, did you know that I got a new job?"

I forced a smile, trying to push away my gloomy thoughts.

"That's great. Where?"

"Over at the Astro Lounge. I'm bartending fulltime and it's a much classier place than Club 6. A new building with no ghosts attached, and more importantly, no cage."

I laughed.

"Congrats, Paloma," I said, giving her hand a squeeze. "That's really great."

"Yeah," she said. "I think it'll be good for me. It's time I moved on and took my bartending career a little more seriously anyway."

We talked a little longer before I had to leave for work. She invited Ty and me to stop by the Astro Lounge anytime and drinks would be on her. I told her that I was planning a fall party next month and wanted to invite her and her sister.

"Oh, you know there was something I never got a chance to ask you," I said. "There were more important things going on at the time."

"What?"

"At some point you said, 'You don't know me from Adam's house cat.' What does that mean?"

She squinted at me for a moment.

"Oh, yeah," she said. "I don't really know. I think it was just something I picked up at Club 6. Sounds like a Southern expression."

"Well, I'm glad I do know you from Adam's house cat," I said.

She smiled.

I checked my watch and saw that I was running late. I stood up to leave. She got up and gave me another hug.

"I'll see you soon," I said, walking away.

"Abby?" I heard her say. I turned around.

"Yeah?"

"Thanks again for what you did. I mean it."

I waved goodbye.

It wasn't me, I repeated in my head.

I turned away and walked to the Jeep, thinking of Jesse.

Chapter 51

As the weeks passed, I poured more and more of my energy into soccer. I was up to running six miles on the track, four times a week, and I found time to practice every day. There was a sadness in me I couldn't shake, but I could make sure I exhausted myself to the point where I didn't dwell on it. I began sleeping again, all the way through the night.

As we headed into the playoffs, I was playing the best I had since my high school days. Since before my accident, when I had been college material.

The last game of the season was just a formality, a chance to fine tune a few things, rest key players, and build our confidence. But, of course, this being rec soccer, the last refuge of has-beens and never-weres and all lost souls trying to recapture their glory days, everyone treated it like it was life and death. Including me.

We demolished the other team, which was also playoff bound, 5-0. Everything I touched was gold. I assisted on two of the goals and scored the other three.

But as the rest of the team celebrated when it was over, I walked off the field with a hollow feeling. There was no one there to see it. No one I really cared about. Kate was working late. I barely saw Ty anymore. He hadn't come to a game in several weeks. And Jesse.

Jesse wasn't there either. Not like he had been for my only other hat trick all those years ago.

I got into the Jeep and drove away through the dark night, a lump as big as the desert growing in my throat.

Chapter 52

"It's killing me to see you this way, Abby Craig."

I shrugged. I helped a customer, told Lyle the order, and slowly walked to the back to get more napkins. David was still waiting for me when I returned.

"Breakups are such a bitch," he said.

"It's not official yet," I said. "He's still thinking about it."

But it sure felt official.

"Well, I say we put him on the clock," David said. "Tick tock, tick tock. He can't leave you in limbo like this. It's already November! We give him until Thanksgiving to shape up or you, Abby Craig, will ship out. I have tons of hot guys I could set you up with."

I was too tired to even think of a funny response. I looked at the clock. Six and a half hours to go.

"I can't do inventory. Would you mind if I stayed out here at the register?"

"Of course not," he said.

David reached over and gave me a long, genuine hug.

"You'll be okay," he said. "We all go through it."

I sighed and faked a smile as a lady walked up and handed me a piece of paper.

"There's eleven drinks there," she said, her face as sharp as her tone.

Those were always the hardest orders, when one cus-tomer handed us a list. It threw everything off. And even though David stayed up front to help, by the time we fin-ished with her, the line was backed up to the door.

I helped the two moms coming from an exercise class while David took an order from the college professor who was a regular and liked to talk a lot.

I looked up again, my heart dropping out of my chest.

He was in the back of the line, smiling at me.

Adjusting his baseball cap.

THE END

The adventure continues…

44 Book Six

Coming November 2012

ABOUT THE AUTHOR

Like her main character, Jools Sinclair lives in Bend, Oregon. She is currently working on *44 Book Six* as well as the first volume of a new series.

Learn more about Jools Sinclair
and the *44* series at…

JoolsSinclair44.blogspot.com

Made in United States
Orlando, FL
03 December 2024

54921112R00117